GR0 AUG16

'B' ',' ';'

M

'I'

'I'
u

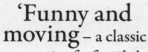
'
bu

''

'Natasha Farrant is exceptional at capturing the details of family life and the swirling emo surroun
Julia Eccleshare

'Funny and moving – a classic

FABER & FABER

has published children's books since 1929. Some of our very first publications included *Old Possum's Book of Practical Cats* by T. S. Eliot, starring the now world-famous Macavity, and *The Iron Man* by Ted Hughes. Our catalogue at the time said that 'it is by reading such books that children learn the difference between the shoddy and the genuine'. We still believe in the power of reading to transform children's lives.

About the Author

Natasha Farrant has worked in children's publishing for almost twenty years, running her own literary scouting agency for the past ten. She is the author of the Carnegie-longlisted and Branford Boase-shortlisted YA historical novel *The Things We Did For Love*, as well as two successful adult novels. Natasha was shortlisted for the Queen of Teen Award 2014, and the second Bluebell Gadbsy book, *Flora in Love*, was longlisted for the Guardian Children's Fiction Prize.

She grew up in London where she still lives with her husband, their two daughters and a large, tortoiseshell cat. She is the eldest of four.

BY THE SAME AUTHOR

The Bluebell Gadsby series
After Iris
Flora in Love
All About Pumpkin

The Things We Did For Love

Natasha Farrant

FABER & FABER

First published in 2016
by Faber & Faber Limited
Bloomsbury House,
74–77 Great Russell Street,
London WC1B 3DA

Typeset by MRules

Printed by CPI Group (UK) Ltd, Croydon CRO 4YY

A CIP record for this book
is available from the British Library

ISBN 978–0–571–32233–6

FSC
www.fsc.org
MIX
Paper from
responsible sources
FSC® C101712

2 4 6 8 10 9 7 5 3 1

For Alice Swan.

And for Lise, who loved
London and its galleries.

THE DIARIES OF BLUEBELL GADSBY

VOLUME 4

TIME FOR JAS

(being a combination of classic diary
entries and transcripts shot by the
author on the video camera given to
her on her 13th birthday)

The Film Diaries of Bluebell Gadsby

Scene One
The Appearance of a Zebra

Daytime, Chatsworth Square (West London home of the Gadsby family, newly returned from their summer holiday in Devon).

Three children are playing a ball game in the street. They are TWIG GADSBY (twelve, still brown from his holidays, wearing mismatched trainers because he forgot one each of two pairs at his grandmother's in Devon), DODI CARTWRIGHT (fourteen, but impeccable as ever in white shorts and a grey sequinned tank top) and JASMINE GADSBY (ten, barefoot because her flip flops keep falling off, tangled hair because she never brushes it, torn too-small dress because it's her favourite).

The game consists of throwing a ball at each other as hard as possible. With the exception of the Gadsby family's scruffy-looking house, this is a very smart neighbourhood, and not the sort in which children run about throwing things and shouting.

Flowers have been trampled. Injuries sustained. A plant pot has been broken.

TWIG
(jumps up from behind a BMW
convertible and hurls the ball at
Dodi)
Take that, rat!

DODI
(dives behind a bank of tall purple
flowers in Mrs Henderson's front
garden, taking off one of their heads
as she goes)
Not this time, pig!

JASMINE
(jumps up and down, screaming)
Throw it to me! Throw it to me!

Dodi is a terrible thrower, especially when she is laughing. The ball doesn't simply miss Jasmine. It sails from Dodi's hands in the opposite direction, straight towards where CAMERAMAN (BLUEBELL, fourteen, denim cut-offs, falling apart sneakers, shoulder-length plaits and glasses) sits filming the game on the roof of the Gadsby family's battered people carrier. Cameraman ducks. The ball misses her, bounces on the car bonnet and rolls into the gutter.

Picture jumps about as Cameraman slides off car roof and crouches on edge of pavement to retrieve the ball. She utters exclamation of surprise.

TWIG
Blue, the ball!

Blue ignores him and resumes filming. There is the tarmac road, the contrasting stone edging of the gutter. Black rubber tires, discarded litter and . . .

CAMERAMAN
A *zebra*?

The car was parked over a drain cover, the rectangular kind with a grid for rainwater to run into. The dull, brown kind you would never normally notice, except that today someone had used chalks to colour the grid in black and white zebra stripes, with a head and four legs, a stripy mane and tail AND A BLUEBELL IN ITS MOUTH.

A *bluebell*.

Just to be clear: a bluebell *like my name*.

I stared at the zebra/drain. It stared back. The others shouted for the ball. I nearly told them to come and look, but something stopped me.

It was so ... weird. And pretty. And somehow – because of the bluebell – private.

'Blue, the *ball!*' Twig shouted from across the street, and then Mrs Henderson came out of her house shouting about her flowers and what did we think we were doing?

The real reason for the ball game is that Twig is starting secondary school next week, and he's worried he's going to be rubbish at sport. Twig is easily the cleverest person in our family. He knows everything there is to know about things like science and natural history, but he is not very coordinated physically, and he thinks that now that he is going to a big school everyone will laugh at him if he can't even catch a ball. I have tried to explain it doesn't matter, and that I have been at Clarendon Free for years without being good at sports, but he says it's different for boys and he doesn't want people to think he's a nerd and please could we just practise as much as possible. I did think of telling Mrs Henderson, who is quite a nice person when she's not cross, but by now a group of people had gathered nearby.

There was a dark-haired boy about my age and a little round man I had never seen before, both in spotless white and clutching tennis rackets, and Mrs Doriot-Buffet, the big American lady who moved in at the beginning of summer, dressed in a turquoise velvet tracksuit and trying to stop her fat black and tan miniature dachshund getting tangled up in its lead as it went round and round in circles.

'I think it's trying to do a poo,' Jas remarked loudly.

The boy stifled a laugh. The little round man smacked him on the arm. Mrs Doriot-Buffet flushed and said how sorry she was for poor Mrs Henderson's hydrangeas. The little round man said *his* son would *never* behave like that. The boy's hair flopped over his face as he stared at the pavement.

'We're extremely sorry,' I started to say, but then Flora burst out of our house with a naked Pumpkin on her hip and her dress covered in mashed food, yelling at us to come indoors THIS MINUTE for lunch.

Mrs Doriot-Buffet stared at her, horrified.

'She probably thinks Pumpkin is Flora's baby,' Dodi grinned before she left us.

'Don't leave us alone with her,' I begged, but Dodi said there was no way she was staying if Flora was cooking.

The situation at home is this: Mum's maternity leave is over, but as usual she has left it too late to get organised and find a nanny. Flora doesn't leave for drama school for a while, so she is in charge of looking after Pumpkin and, supposedly, us. This means she thinks she can shout at us as much as she wants, and also feed us the same mashed-up baby food Pumpkin eats now he doesn't just drink milk.

We have all begged our ex-nanny Zoran to look after us instead, but he is leaving London soon for Devon with his glamorous girlfriend Gloria. She is in the middle of selling her riding school under the motorway not far from here, after which she will move all her ponies to Grandma's house to create the

Horsehill School of Riding, while Zoran composes songs on Grandma's piano and gives music lessons and looks after Grandma because she is getting too old to live in a big house all by herself. Dad can't help because he is staying in Devon until Zoran and Gloria move, and also because he is hopeless, and the one time he looked after Pumpkin all day on his own he left him in the park because he was so busy thinking about the book he is writing.

'What vegetable is it today?' Twig asked, as Flora served up dollops of slop.

'Broccoli.'

'It's *brown*.'

Flora said that was because she added Nutella to make it sweeter, and he should stop complaining or she'd tell Mum about us trampling Mrs Henderson's garden. Jas and Twig made gagging noises all through lunch. I tried to be polite, but gave up after about three spoonfuls.

'I saw this amazing drawing of a zebra,' I said. Now that I'd got over the surprise, I wanted to ask them to come out and look at the drawing. 'It was the weirdest thing. Someone had drawn it on a drain, and it had . . .'

I wasn't so sure any more if the flower *was* a bluebell, and I wanted them to tell me if *they* thought it was, and if it meant anything or was it just coincidence that someone had drawn a picture of a flower that was *my* name under *our* car.

Then Pumpkin threw his bowl on the floor, and Jas laughed so hard she spat water all over the table. Flora shouted, 'Zebras! I'm already surrounded by animals!'

It was hopeless trying to get their attention. Instead, I took my camera out to the garden and looked at it again and again.

The flower in the zebra's mouth has a green stalk and a cluster of blue, bell-like petals. It is most definitely a bluebell.

Thursday 2 September

Zoran called yesterday to say he had a friend who wouldn't mind being our nanny, and he brought her this afternoon to meet us. Her name is Pixie O'Dare, she has just arrived in London from Ireland to make money to pay to go travelling, and she is possibly the prettiest person I have ever seen. She is tiny, with wrists as small as Jas's, an upturned nose with a dusting of freckles, a mouth like a strawberry, green eyes with thick black lashes and a page-boy cut with a bleached blonde crown graduating through shades of pink to bright bubble-gum at the tips. She was dressed in a navy boiler suit, but her toe and fingernails were painted with glitter, and on her back she was wearing . . . wings.

Actual, glittery wings.

Zoran started to introduce us. Pumpkin, who hates not being the centre of attention, did that thing where he goes from giggling to screaming in about two seconds. Pixie held out her arms. Flora handed him over. Pumpkin instantly stopped crying, which *was* impressive, because the fastest anyone has ever got him to stop screaming is one minute and seventeen seconds, when Jas held him right up in a horse's face in Devon and he was so astonished he practically stopped breathing. I thought maybe Jas would be jealous, but she just frowned like she was a bit puzzled, and asked Pixie why she was wearing wings.

Pixie said, because you should always wear clothes that make you happy. She waggled her shoulders. The wings fluttered, and Jas laughed.

'You see?' Pixie said.

Then Flora asked, why was she wearing a boiler suit. Pixie said they were the best thing for looking after babies, and to just look at Flora's dress.

'What's wrong with my dress?' Flora asked.

'You'll never get that mash out. This boiler suit, now. This is heavy duty.'

Flora wrinkled her nose, because she doesn't like other people being better at clothes than she is. She actually used to have pink hair too, but it didn't look as good as Pixie's, and I could tell she was annoyed about the wings as well as the boiler suit, because it's true that even though Pixie did look a bit mad, the whole combination somehow worked.

Jas was so impressed she made up a poem on the spot – *Pixie O'Dare, so pink and fair, I love the way she does her hair, Her skills with babies can't compare, To anybody's in the square.* Pixie said what a lovely poem and she couldn't wait to hear more of Jas's work. Flora barged in and said *she* was going to drama school, and then she explained all about how exclusive the Foulkes-Watson School for the Performing Arts is, and how it's in a big country house in Scotland, and how she was in a film last summer.

'A real film,' Flora said. 'Not like the ones Blue makes.'

'My films *are* real!' I protested, but then Mum came home and no-one could get a word in edgeways, between Pumpkin squealing and Jas reciting her

11

Pixie poem and Twig practising throwing and catching and Flora announcing loudly that she was going to go to the hairdresser tomorrow and maybe get her hair dyed ORANGE.

Jas spent the evening throwing out all the clothes she says don't make her happy. Twig and I watched leggings and jumpers pile up on the floor.

'I like that,' I said, pointing at a brown wool cardigan.

'Dull!' Jas cried, with her head in her wardrobe. 'You can have it if you want.'

'Thanks,' I said, but she didn't get the sarcasm.

'What do *you* think of Pixie?' Twig asked.

'Odd,' I said. 'But good with Pumpkin. What do you think?'

'I think she's fine, but I don't want her coming anywhere near my school.'

Friday 3 September

Flora did go to the hairdresser this morning (she has had a perm, and her hair is so curly it sticks out almost horizontally all around her head so that she looks like a sheep). I looked after Pumpkin while she was gone. Dodi came round and we lay in the garden in the sun, with Pumpkin rolling about on a blanket in the shade and Dodi going on and on about Jake while I pondered the Mystery of the Chalk Drawing.

Dodi and Jake have been going out since March, if you count the whole of August when they didn't see each other, and he is beginning to get on her nerves.

'He messaged me every day while I was in Spain,' she said. 'Every single day! And not like interesting stuff. Just "hi" and "miss you" and "thinking about you, *happy face*" and the first time I saw him after I got back he brought flowers. Flowers! Not even nice ones – tulips, that went all droopy. He wants to take me to a theme park for my birthday. I told him, my birthday's not till *June* and he was like, I know but it's cheaper if you book early . . .'

All the time Dodi was talking, I was thinking about the zebra. 'It is a perfectly logical thing to draw on a stripy drain cover,' I reflected. 'If you were going to turn a drain cover into anything, a zebra is the best thing you could do. The question is, *why do you do it in the first place?* And why do you draw a *bluebell*?'

Dodi kicked me. I started.

'Sorry,' I said, and tried to pay more attention.

Being back in London feels very different to being on holiday in Devon. In Devon there is Skye, who even though I only met him this summer is the sort of friend who actually listens to me. And there is Grandma, who even though she is ill and forgetful also pays attention to me. At home, the only one who ever used to listen was Iris. That was the thing about having a twin sister. I mattered to her. Even though she always preferred things like climbing and animals to books and drawings, I know she would have been interested in the zebra because she knew it was important to me.

But Iris has been dead for four years now, and quite frankly sometimes I think I could paint my naked body blue and jump up and down screaming and still no-one would listen.

Today, when Mum came home from work, the whole house was taken over by the argument of what Flora should take to Scotland.

'It will be cold.' Mum dumped a load of thermal underwear on Flora's bed.

'I'm not wearing it!' Flora declared. 'It's the sort of thing Grandma wears. Those knickers probably *are* Grandma's. I bet actual live Scottish people don't wear thermal underwear. I bet they'd rather die of frostbite.'

'If you wear them,' Mum said, 'you will not die of frostbite.'

'I would rather my nose dropped off!' Flora cried.

Twig said surely Flora would not wear thermal knickers on her nose. Flora started to shout at him, but then Dad skyped from Devon and Flora asked did *he* think she should take the underwear to Scotland? Dad said, 'What are you talking about? Here, speak to your grandmother' and then Grandma appeared on the screen and said of course Flora should, and personally she swore by thermal underwear.

Flora got very grumpy and said everyone was ganging up against her, but the fact is that she is so excited about drama school nothing can really dent her good mood for long. All through dinner (which was pasta and ketchup because she used the money Mum left for shopping on her hair), she kept telling us what an amazing time she is going to have, until Twig grumbled anyone would think she was the only one starting a new school.

'I'm starting YEAR SEVEN,' he said, but Flora ignored him.

Mum sighed and said she couldn't believe how fast we were all growing up.

'It's a very important year for me too,' Jas reminded her, and Mum agreed that the last year of primary school was *extremely* important.

'We're going to start a poetry club,' Jas said. 'Miss Jamison said last term she thought it was an excellent idea. *Excellent*. Miss Jamison loves poetry because she's a librarian.'

By the time Mum finally said, 'What about you, Blue? What's special for you this year?' she looked exhausted, and I was pretty certain she couldn't cope with chalk zebras and bluebells. Instead I just said, 'I've got exams this year,' which made her look instantly guilty for not remembering.

Later on, I called Skye in Devon and told *him* about the zebra. He listened, just as I knew he would.

'It was just there, looking at me,' I said. 'Underneath *our car*. With a *bluebell* in its mouth.'

'Is that creepy?'

I thought about it for a moment. How do I feel about this zebra?

'It's intriguing,' I said at last.

Skye said, 'Well let me know if you see any more. You know, if the zebra turns into a herd and starts galloping about the streets of London,' and we both sniggered.

I love Skye. I wish he wasn't so far away. Or that we lived in Devon.

Mum came in as I finished talking, and I could tell she was relieved to see me laughing.

'I didn't want you to think I'd forgotten about your exams,' she said.

'I know,' I said. 'Honestly Mum, it's fine. I know how busy you are.'

She hugged me and said, like she always does, 'Thank heavens for my sensible Blue.'

My phone pinged as she left the room. It was a message from Skye, with a picture of a zebra baring its teeth and the caption *bluebells are my favourite food*.

'Very funny,' I wrote back.

I really do hate it when Mum calls me sensible.

The Film Diaries of
Bluebell Gadsby

Scene Two
Flowers on the Way
to School

Blenheim Avenue, eight o'clock in the
morning. Cars, vans, delivery trucks,
taxis and red double-decker buses crawl
through rush-hour traffic. Bicycles,
scooters and motorbikes weave around
them. The weather is fine again after
a rainy weekend, but it is clear that
summer is over. The sun is lower, the
light softer. The sun shines but there
is a chill in the air. People wear
cardigans and jackets.

The street is crowded with all
manner of people: men in suits and
overalls and hard hats, women in heels
and sneakers and work dresses and
jeans, women veiled, women in saris,

black skin, white skin, everything in between skin, people talking English, Polish, French, Spanish, Hindi, Czech and Arabic, people pushing babies in buggies and dragging toddlers, crowding bus stops and disappearing underground to the Tube, with takeout cups and briefcases and dogs of all shapes and sizes, dachshunds and collies and spaniels and terriers, on leads, on chains, on pieces of string. Squirrels scoot along trees. Pigeons flap. Cats skulk.

Today is the first day back at school. Children in different uniforms drag their feet in bundled groups along the pavement. Red and black, grey-tipped navy, bottle green. Primary kids in brightly coloured sweatshirts, Year Sevens squeaky clean with too-big blazers and skirts just the right length and brand new school bags, older kids looking scuffed and knocked about, with rolled-up skirts and battered rucksacks and buttons undone as far as they dare.

DODI, TWIG and JASMINE walk along Blenheim Avenue, their lack of uniform marking them out as Clarendon Free School students.

Dodi is impeccable as ever in her first day outfit of skinny jeans, suede sneakers and a flowery bomber jacket. Twig wears shorts, shiny new trainers and a hoody. Jas, inspired by Pixie, is wearing her favourite happy clothes: her ripped, too-short summer dress, freshly washed for the occasion, over purple leggings and silver high-tops and under an old lacy cardigan of Flora's, her mane of wild black hair tied high on her head by a rainbow-striped ribbon.

CAMERAMAN (BLUEBELL, in jeans, trainers and an oversized grey sweatshirt she thought was cute but is now worried just looks like it's her dad's) films as she follows, walking very slowly.

Two primary school twin girls walk past in bright red sweatshirts and pigtails. One skips, swinging her satchel. The other scowls and shuffles, then stops walking completely.

PIGTAILED GIRL
Why do I have to go to school?

Camera zooms in on her stamping foot, then follows pavement to where it opens into a narrow alley between two buildings, just wide enough for the blue transit van which blocks its entry. There is less than a foot of space between the sides of the van and the walls of the buildings, and that space is dark and full of shadows. Nobody would think of looking at it, but something – a flash of unexpected colour – has caught Cameraman's eye.

She crouches beside the van, adjusts lighting, zooms in on the wall on the left-hand side. She walks around the front of the van and does the same on the other side.

Both walls are covered in chalk drawings of bluebells.

The first spring after Iris died, Grandma took me to see the bluebells near Horsehill. It was a special expedition just for me. She came to get me in London all the way from Devon, and she took me back with her on the train even though it was a school day, because she said I had to see them when they were perfect. 'It's like seeing the sea under the trees,' she said.

I had no idea what she meant until we got there, but then I understood immediately. It was like a whole ocean of flowers, a swaying cloud of delicate blue, bright and luminous in the gloom of the forest. 'Every year, they come back,' Grandma whispered as we watched, and I knew it was her way of telling me that life goes on.

The bluebells on the walls were the same. Not so much 'life goes on', but 'look how pretty even this old wall can be if you just try'. There are thin cracks along the bottom of the walls, full of earth blown in from the street, tufts of grass and weeds like dandelions. The artist has drawn the flowers like they're growing out of them, following the lines of the real plants so it looks like the bluebells are growing up the bricks, before turning into a sea of blue like the flowers in the wood near Grandma's. They looked so real I put down my camera and reached out to touch them. Blue chalk came off on my hand. I stared at it, my mind whirring.

Bluebells.

I could have stood there for ages, but Dodi marched back to get me and said she doesn't want me getting detention for being late on the very first day.

'If you're in detention,' she said, 'I'll have to walk home with Jake.'

'Look!' I pointed at the flowers, but she was already walking away. I wiped my hands on my sweatshirt and ran after her.

We dropped Jas off at the primary school. Twig, looking a bit green, went off to the gym to join all the other Year Sevens, while Dodi and I stayed in the schoolyard to wait for Jake.

We – me, Dodi, Jake and his best friends Colin and Tom – are all in the same form again. Miss Foundry is our form tutor and is teaching us English, but because this year we get to choose our own subjects, we're not together for everything.

Dodi, as usual, knows what everybody is doing.

'All together for English,' she announced at lunchtime, waving our timetables about. 'And

Maths. Jake and Colin are together for Geography, me and Tom and Blue have History, Jake and Tom have French when me and Colin and Blue do Spanish, and Tom is the only one doing art.'

There's a new boy in our form, and she grabbed his subject list as he walked past our table and worked out when we have classes with him, too.

'We can show you where to go,' she said kindly.

'Ignore her,' Tom advised him. 'Or she'll rule your life.'

Jake, who had been gazing lovingly at Dodi all through her announcements, said not to talk to Poodle like that.

I said, '*Poodle?*'

Dodi glared at everyone like she was daring us to laugh.

I didn't recognise the new boy at first. His name is Marek Valenta and he is very pale with black hair perfectly parted on one side. He was dressed like a sort of expensive European model in pressed jeans, a soft leather jacket, a pale blue shirt and loafers. In form he sat right at the front, listened to everything Miss Foundry said, took lots of notes and didn't speak to anybody all morning, except to Hattie Verney when she asked him where he was before Clarendon Free and he said 'Prague', which is in the Czech Republic.

But then, at lunch, when everyone was laughing at Dodi and Jake and the whole Poodle thing, he quietly took back his timetable. His hair flopped forward as he shoved it in his school bag, and I remembered where I had seen him before.

'You were in the square the other day!' I said. 'You'd been playing tennis!'

The new boy didn't look at me but stared at my chalk-covered, too-big sweatshirt in a way that made me worry all over again about how scruffy I looked.

'There was a dog!' I insisted to cover up my embarrassment. 'A dachshund, going round and round, trying to do a ...'

Now the others were all laughing at me.

Tom asked, 'What exactly was the dog trying to do?' while Jake and Colin started going round and round in circles pretending to sniff each other's bottoms.

'It *was* him,' I insisted as the new boy walked away, and I think Tom felt sorry for me, because he told the others to stop.

Tom has changed. He's grown, for a start. He looks about a foot taller than before the holidays, and he's got lots of spots, but he behaves like he doesn't even know they're there and also like he's not just part of the Jake–Colin–Tom trio any more, but an actual separate person. He walked part of the way home with us after school. I thought of showing him the flowers, but when we went past they had already been washed away.

At dinner tonight (scrambled eggs and mashed potato), Mum was very careful to ask me first about my day, and I was very careful not to tell her about the bluebell field. If I did, and she actually listened, I am almost sure there would be a fuss. That is the way with my family – all or nothing. Then, if I told her about the bluebells today, I would probably end up saying about the zebra, and even though I do often wish I got more attention, there is a strong chance that instead of saying, 'Darling, how lovely,' she would freak out about stalkers or something. And then Flora would chip in with either, 'Ooh, Blue's got an admirer' or, 'Why would anyone stalk *her?*' and it would all be completely exhausting.

So instead I said, 'I got my timetable,' and then she moved on to Twig and asked about his first day at school and he said 'fine', quite cautiously, like he hadn't made up his mind yet if he liked it or not, and then Jas stuck her jaw out the way she does when she's decided something and said, 'There's an art competition at school, just for Year Six. It's got a theme and everything. The theme is: the Circle of Life.'

'Like in *The Lion King*?' Twig asked. 'What does that even mean?'

Jas said she didn't know about *The Lion King*, but that Mr Boniface, the art teacher, says that it's all about nature, and things dying but then coming to life again, like flowers after the winter.

Like bluebells, I thought.

'I didn't know you were interested in art,' Mum said.

'I'm not,' Jas said. 'I'm interested in winning.'

Thursday 9 September

Pixie moved in last night. This morning, when I came down for breakfast Mum had already left for work, and Pixie was standing on a purple mat in the kitchen with her eyes closed and the baby monitor next to her and the palms of her hands pressed together in front of her chest.

'It's yoga,' Twig explained. 'Apparently she does it every morning.'

Pixie let out a huge breath like a cat hissing, and folded in two, grabbing hold of her toes. Upstairs, Pumpkin was waking up. We heard him gurgle through the baby monitor. Pixie peered at us through a gap between her knees.

'Should I go?' she asked.

The monitor crackled, and Jas begin to sing.

Hush little baby don't you cry-ooh
Jas ain't going nowhere
She's going to stay right here by-you
If you say a little prayer

'Bless.' Pixie smiled, like it was the cutest thing ever.

'She wrote that herself,' Twig told her.

Pixie said again how talented Jas is. My phone pinged. It was Dodi, saying we were late and she couldn't wait for us. I looked at the time and cried, 'We have to go to school!'

'School?' Pixie looked baffled.

'We're going to be late!'

'Late?'

I think maybe Pixie is only really good at looking after babies.

The singing on the monitor started again.

Jas is gonna stay home all day
Looking after you
We're just gonna laugh and play
Nobody'll be blue

'JAS!' I went out into the garden and shouted up at Pumpkin's window. The singing stopped. Pumpkin started to cry. Jas appeared, still in her nightie, and flung the window open.

'Now see what you've done!' she yelled. 'He was happy a second ago.'

Pixie and Twig came out into the garden. We all stood there in a row, looking up at Jas.

'You're not dressed!' I shouted.

'I'm not going to school today. Mum said I didn't have to.'

'Did she really?' Twig asked. Pixie scrunched up her face and said she didn't remember Mum saying anything about school at all.

In my head, I heard Mum saying, '*Thank goodness for my sensible Blue*'. I shan't say a word, I thought. It's none of my business if she goes to school or not.

'You can't bunk off in your first week.' Flora appeared at the window next to Jas, yawning, her curly hair standing up on end from being slept on, and said she totally sympathised with Jas, that only swots and idiots liked school but that it was less boring than staying at home all day, that Jas could borrow any clothes she wanted and when she was ready, Flora would take her in.

'Any clothes at all?' Jas asked. Flora said yes. Jas

went inside to dress, and Twig and I ran all the way to school. By the time we arrived I was pink and sweaty and the tiny bit of eye makeup I'd put on this morning was running down my face from under my glasses. The new boy in his perfectly ironed jeans stared at me like I came from another planet. Dodi rolled her eyes, handed me a face wipe and a hand-mirror and said next time I should try using waterproof mascara.

'I will never in a million years look as sophisticated as her,' I complained to Skye this afternoon on the phone. 'She's my best friend, but she makes me feel like a scruffy little kid.'

Skye said scruffy people were his favourite kind. I think he was trying to help, but it didn't make me feel any better.

Saturday 11 September

Marek Valenta came to our house this evening for a drink with his parents. Mum met his mother in the supermarket and invited them.

'I thought it would be a nice neighbourly thing to do,' she said when I protested. 'They've only just arrived here from Prague.'

'But he's in my form!' I said.

'All the more reason to invite him,' Mum said. 'You can be friends.'

'He keeps looking at my clothes.'

Mum said she had no idea what I was talking about and please could I go to the shop to buy crisps.

Marek Valenta looks just like his mother, who is English and pale with dark hair and eyes, but you can tell he's his father son just by the way he dresses. I think they are both a bit afraid of Mr Valenta, who looks like a robin and talks with a heavy East European accent and never lets either of them speak.

Dad says Mr Valenta is tremendously rich, and has moved his company from Prague to London in order to get even richer. His trousers are perfectly creased, his shirt perfectly ironed under a navy blue blazer, he wears a maroon dotted cravat round his neck and he likes talking about how rich he is. Mum admired his hat and he told her it was custom made for him in Paris.

'And my brogues were hand-stitched in Italy!' Mr Valenta beamed, showing two gold teeth that are probably encrusted with diamonds. 'Only the best will do!'

Dad, who has come home for a few days from looking after Grandma in Devon, tugged at the sleeve of his cardigan to hide the holes at the elbows.

Mrs Valenta, who looked very posh in a silk dress and heels but is much nicer than her husband, said how pretty our piano was and asked who played.

Mum said, no-one since our ex-nanny Zoran moved out. Mrs Valenta said her husband used to play the violin.

'Extremely well, actually,' She said. 'He was accepted at the Conservatoire in Prague. He wanted to be a professional musician.'

A funny look passed between them at that moment. Mr Valenta looked annoyed, but also lost – like he hadn't expected her to say what she did, and had no idea how to react. She gazed back at him looking nervous but also defiant, like she was daring him to react.

It was so quick, I don't think anyone else noticed. Then Mr Valenta laughed.

'But there was no money in it!' He waved his hand to dismiss all talk of pianos and violins, and went back to his lecture about clothes. 'I see these young people at Marek's school, with their dirty jeans and their hoods on their heads. How can you learn, dressed like that, hmm?' He swept us with an imperious gaze. Dad tugged at his cardigan again. 'I wanted Marek to go to the proper British boarding school, with suits and shirts and ties. St Llwydian. It is in Wales – do you know it? The pupils run ten miles every day before breakfast to be fit and strong. But he begged me no. *I want to be normal, Tata. I do not want to do the running or wear the shirts and ties. I want to stay in London which reminds me of Prague.* Fine, I said. Go to school with the hoody boys, but if your grades or behaviour are ANYTHING SHORT OF EXEMPLARY...' – everyone's eyes turned to his upheld finger – 'it is off to St Llwydian with you! Eh, Marek?'

'Yes, Tata.'

I don't think a single one of us would have stood Mum or Dad talking to us like that for one second, but Marek didn't so much as blink.

'Do you miss Prague, Marek?' Mum asked gently.

'Yes.' Marek blushed as he replied, and didn't dare look at his father. 'Yes, I do. Very much.'

'I would like to go to boarding school,' Jas said thoughtfully. 'If it was like the Chalet School or Hogwarts. I think it would be infinitely better than real school.'

Mr Valenta squinted at her and asked what she was talking about. Mum explained they were boarding schools in books. Mr Valenta said he was pleased to hear that Jas was a reader, but he hoped stories didn't get in the way of her schoolwork and said that Marek here didn't waste his time reading for pleasure, did he?

'No, Tata.'

Jas glared at Mr Valenta. Upstairs, Pumpkin started to cry. Mum nudged her. Jas left, still glaring, but Marek's father had turned his attention to Flora, asking if she was off to university.

Flora said she was going to drama school.

'There's no money in acting,' Mr Valenta declared. 'Not unless you make it to the very top. Are you going to make it to the very top, young lady?'

Flora said probably, yes. Mum said that what mattered to her and Dad was that their children were happy.

'Happy!' Mr Valenta nearly choked laughing. 'They will be happy if they are successful, and they will be successful if they are rich.'

Mum said she thought success shouldn't be measured by how rich you were, but by how fulfilling your life was. Mr Valenta didn't listen.

'For example, you ...' He pointed at me. 'Did I or did I not see you the other day, sitting on a car filming a ball game in the street?'

Marek started, but when I looked at him he was doing his usual thing of staring at the floor with his hair over his eyes.

'Blue is interested in making documentaries,' Mum said. Her voice was shorter than usual, but

Mr Valenta didn't notice.

'Documentaries!' he cried. 'My, my, my.'

Dad, who had been turning various shades of red throughout this conversation, knocked back his whisky and poured himself another. Flora looked at me and rolled her eyes. I rolled mine back. Twig pressed his lips together like he was trying not to laugh. Jas came back in, carrying a wailing Pumpkin.

'He's got another tooth coming through and it's making his bottom red,' she announced.

Twig snorted. Flora handed him a tissue as his eyes started to water. Mr Valenta said he didn't believe in babies being allowed downstairs after seven o'clock.

Jas said, 'How would *you* like to be stuck in a room all on your own if *your* bottom was sore?'

Twig exploded and ran out of the room to laugh his head off on the landing where he thought we couldn't hear him. Mrs Valenta said she thought perhaps they should go. Mum agreed that it was getting late.

'Well!' she said, as the door closed behind them.

Dad cried, 'Please promise me you will never invite those people here again?'

'Shh!' Flora was standing by the open window. Outside, Mr Valenta was still holding forth.

'A most unusual family,' he was saying. 'Not the sort of neighbours one was expecting, not people like us at all.'

'No, dear.'

'I hope you are not friends with them, Marek.'

'No, Tata.'

They moved on, out of earshot.

'Not people like us at all.'

Flora's imitation was perfect. We laughed so hard our tummies hurt, but still – no wonder Marek Valenta is the way he is.

'Poor kid,' Flora said later, as we finished up the crisps. 'No-one should be made to dress like that.'

'I'd go to Wales like a shot if my dad was like that,' Twig said. 'In fact, I'd quite like to go to Wales anyway.' His eyes shone, and I knew he must be thinking about some rare birds, or animals, or rock formation they have there.

'Boarding school,' Jas sighed.

'Ten miles of running a day,' Flora reminded her. 'Rather him than me.'

After they'd gone, Dad insisted we had takeaway pizza for dinner, and we ate it straight from the box on the living room floor in front of the TV.

'I bet *Mr Valenta* doesn't do this,' he gloated through a dripping mouthful of cheese.

I imagined them all sitting down to dinner across the square. They probably have a huge dining room like the ones you see in films set in castles or something, with straight-backed chairs and acres and acres of gleaming table between them, and different knives and forks depending on what they're eating.

'You've got tomato sauce on your chin,' Jas informed me.

I rubbed it away and licked my fingers. It was delicious.

Definitely rather him than me, I thought.

Tuesday 14 September

Zoran came round on his way home from teaching a music lesson. We sat in the garden and he told me that Gloria exchanged contracts yesterday with the people who want to buy her stables.

'We should be moving just before half-term,' he said. 'I thought you would like to know.'

'So you'll be leaving,' I said sadly, and Zoran nudged me with his elbow the way he always does and said, 'Yes, but your father will be coming home then because we will be with your grandmother,' and wasn't that a nice thing, and as I grew up I would understand that life is made up of people coming and going but when you love them, they are somehow always with you.

Zoran is adorable, but he does go on.

Jas came out, balancing a pair of cushions, an A3 drawing pad and Pumpkin in her arms. Zoran hurried to help her.

'What *are* you doing?' he asked.

'Art.'

She wedged Pumpkin between the cushions, sat cross-legged on the grass in front of him and began to draw. Pumpkin gurgled, stuffed his fist in his mouth and lurched slowly sideways until he was lying flat on the mat.

Jas threw down her sketchpad. 'I hate art!'

Zoran asked why didn't Jas try to draw something less wriggly. Jas explained about the art show and the circle of life. 'It was Pixie's idea. Because he's a baby. Pixie believes that when people die, they're born again as something else. She says that's what the circle of life means. It's not just flowers.'

'Wouldn't flowers be easier?' Zoran asked.

'*Everyone* does flowers,' Jas said.

She propped Pumpkin up again. He grinned and this time threw himself back down on the mat with a happy squeal.

'Does it have to be a picture?' Zoran asked. 'Because you could write a poem. You're good at that.'

'A poem's not *art*.'

'The reason art changes people's lives,' Zoran said, 'is that it makes people look at things differently. It's exactly the same with poetry. You could stand up and recite it, and call it performance art.'

'Do you really think that?' I asked.

'That Jas should write a poem?'

'That art changes people's lives?'

'Don't you?'

'I don't know,' I said, but when Zoran left, I walked with him to the end of the road, and then I came back very slowly, looking under cars at every drain cover I passed, and peering into every dark corner, imagining them all turned into flowers and animals.

If I was as good as the chalk artist, I wouldn't hide my drawings under cars or in dark alleys. I would have a huge exhibition on enormous canvases, and invite everyone I know to come and look at it, and post photographs of it all over the internet, and nobody would ever not listen to me again, or tell me what makeup to wear, or that my clothes were boring.

We are studying a book in English called *Of Mice and Men* by an American writer called John Steinbeck. It was on our reading list for the holidays, but when Miss Foundry asked who had read it, only swotty Hattie Verney said she had until Dodi grabbed my hand and shoved it in the air.

'Stop it!' I hissed. 'She'll only make me talk about it!'

I thought Miss Foundry would die on the spot, she was so pleased.

'Bluebell Gadsby!' she cried. 'I knew, among this group of Philistines, I could rely on you!'

Tom smirked. Colin giggled. Jake said, 'What's a Philistine?'

'A Philistine is an uneducated idiot,' Tom said. 'Like you.'

'Come and stand at the front, Blue,' Miss Foundry trilled. 'Tell us all about the book.'

That is exactly why I didn't want to admit to having read the book. Miss Foundry *always* makes us stand at the front. I shuffled up to the white board and turned towards the class. A sea of faces looked back at me.

I cleared my throat. 'It's about . . .'

'Please, Miss!' Hattie was almost falling out of her

chair in her desperation to answer the question, but my mind stayed absolutely blank.

'It's about ...'

I don't know why Flora wants to be an actress, I honestly don't. Standing up to talk in front of people is the worst form of torture that has ever been invented.

Miss Foundry said, 'Bluebell?' but my brain stayed empty.

My eyes fell on the front row, where Marek Valenta was behaving in a most peculiar way.

'I ...'

Marek puffed himself up and out, like he was trying to make himself look really big. Then he drew his finger across his throat and dropped his head to one side with his tongue hanging out, like he was pretending to be dead.

'It's about this big man,' I gasped. 'His name's Lennie. He's like a giant, and he's strong, so strong he keeps killing things by mistake. He doesn't mean to because he's nice, but he kills a mouse, and a puppy, and then a girl, and then his best friend shoots him to stop other people killing *him*.'

Everyone looked shocked, except for Miss Foundry who I think was disappointed by my synopsis.

'It's good,' I added, but it was too late.

'I'm not reading that,' Jake protested.

'Can't we read something cheerful?' Tom asked.

'*Of Mice and Men* is a masterpiece!' Miss Foundry declared.

'Has a book got to be miserable, Miss?' asked Colin. 'To be a masterpiece, I mean?'

'Course it has, stupid,' Jake said. 'Look at Harry Potter.'

'Harry Potter's not a masterpiece,' Hattie said.

'Of course it's a flipping masterpiece!' Jake insisted.

'It's not, Jake. Not like Steinbeck.'

'Then how come everyone's read Harry Potter and no-one's read this mouse book?'

'Class, please!' Miss Foundry cried.

But everyone was shouting at everyone else by then, and I think she knew it was hopeless trying to get our attention. She started to distribute worksheets instead, which we all ignored.

'Thank you,' I whispered to Marek as I walked back to my seat.

He stared down at his desk, but I think I saw him smile.

Flora left for Scotland very early this morning, to her super-exclusive country house theatre school near Glasgow. Dad came home from Devon again especially to take her and last night we had a big farewell dinner for her. Zoran and Gloria came too, and Flora didn't stop showing off all evening.

'Of course, I have already acted in a feature film,' Flora said. 'So I'm probably way ahead of the others already.'

Gloria, who with her tight black clothes and long wavy hair and bright red lipstick looks more like a supermodel than a horse person, said if the school was that exclusive, wouldn't the others have loads of experience too? Flora, who loves Gloria but loves the limelight more, said, 'Yes, but a *feature* film.'

'A feature film I wrote,' Dad commented.

'In which you didn't have any lines,' Twig added.

Flora said she didn't just get that part because Dad wrote it and it didn't matter about the lines, it was her facial expressions that mattered. Pixie said she was sure Flora was absolutely wonderful in Dad's film, she couldn't wait for it to come out and she was sure next time they would let her speak. Flora cried that her part in the film had been *very* important and the great tragedy of her life was being surrounded by people who didn't understand her.

'That's not tragedy,' I said. 'Tragedy is like Lennie in *Of Mice and Men*, who kills everything he loves.'

Flora said we'd be sorry when *she* ended up dead. Twig thought that was so funny he got hiccoughs. Flora gripped her plate like she was trying to stop herself from throwing her chocolate cheesecake at him. Mum took it away from her and gave it to Dad, who started to eat it. Gloria said, why didn't Zoran play something on the piano?

I love it when Zoran plays. Then Flora started singing, all the old songs Zoran likes, things like 'Stormy Weather' and 'My Baby Just Cares for Me', and even though her voice isn't the best, no-one minded because she was happy again. Pumpkin woke up and Mum brought him down, and we all sat in a heap on the sofa, with Mum leaning against Dad on the floor, and then Gloria sang a flamenco song she learned from her Spanish grandmother and it was exactly the sort of evening our family does best.

Just for a minute, I think Flora forgot about her exciting new life, because her voice wobbled when she said goodbye to us all last night. 'Don't get up tomorrow,' she ordered. 'I don't want weepy dawn farewells on the doorstep.' But I heard Dad come

44

up before it was even light to wake her and I got up anyway. I wrapped my duvet round my shoulders and sat on the stairs while they packed the car with bags of clothes and her vintage turntable and boxes of books and records and a new duvet and her favourite pillow and a bicycle and kettle and mugs and a big cake in a tin Mum made for her, until there was no room for anything except her and Dad squeezed into the front.

Mum pulled Flora into a hug and said again about the thermal underwear.

'Mum!'

'I'm going to miss you so much.' Mum started to cry.

'Blue, stop her!' Flora said. 'This is exactly what I didn't want.'

'I'm going to miss you too,' I admitted.

'I'll be back for Christmas.'

'Christmas!'

'Maybe before.'

I shuffled down the stairs and Flora put her arms round my duvet.

'Don't be too much of a dork,' she said.

'Don't be too much of a diva,' I replied.

And then she was leaving, in her fabulous new drama school purple fedora and her fabulous new drama school orange angora coat, perched on top of her fabulous new drama school chunky heeled leopard skin ankle boots, and it felt like all the air was being sucked out of the house.

She turned at the door and dropped into a low curtsey, the sort actresses do when they're taking a curtain call, and started doing that comedy waving with her hand sticking round the door. Mum started to cry again. I tunnelled an arm through my duvet to hug her. The door closed.

'Flora!' Jas appeared on the landing looking like a wild mad animal, her hair even more tangled than usual, her nightie bunched in her hand above her knees as she tore down the stairs.

'Flora!' she shrieked. She threw open the door and ran into the street, where Flora was about to climb into the car. 'Don't go!' she sobbed. 'Please don't go.'

She flung herself in Flora's arms. Flora's eyes met mine over Jas's shoulder and I swear they were wet as well.

'I have to go, Jazzcakes,' she whispered in her ear. Mum took Jas by the hand and prised her away. Flora got in the car.

'Remember what I told you,' she said to Jas. And then they drove away.

*

Flora is the most annoying person in the world to live with. Everywhere she goes, there is mess. The bathroom is covered in half-squeezed tubes of foundation and cotton-wool pads covered in makeup, and the landing is covered with clothes leading right up to her bedroom, and there are damp towels draped over banisters and shoes all over the hall and the smell of her perfume and hairspray everywhere, but that's all gone now.

Jas cried for ages, first with Mum, then, when Mum had to go out, with Pixie.

I thought Pixie would do something Pixieish like yoga, but actually she was quite tough, in a gentle sort of way.

'I don't see why she has to go,' Jas sobbed, and Pixie said that everyone has to leave sometime, because everyone has to grow up and you can't grow up unless you have adventures, and you can't have adventures if you just stay at home.

'Look at me,' Pixie said.

'Are you having an adventure?' Twig asked, and Pixie said she was.

'But you're just here with us.'

'Still an adventure.'

'Do you miss home?' I asked, and Pixie said yes she did, every single day, but the good thing was she didn't realise how much she loved home until she went away.

'So you'll go back,' Jas said.

'In a few years' time, I suppose.'

'A few years!' Jas started crying again and said she didn't see why people needed to grow up at all. Pixie said they just did.

Later, I asked Jas what Flora meant when she said 'Remember what I told you'. Jas said it was nothing.

'You would tell me, wouldn't you, if it was something?' I asked.

'Something like what?'

'I don't know.' I thought of Jas, standing at Pumpkin's window in her nightie. 'Something about school?'

Twig, who was lying on the floor reading a science magazine, snorted something like, 'School is for idiots'. Jas sniffed and said she quite agreed.

'Do you want to talk about it?' I asked.

Jas said, 'Not really', and that I sounded like Mum.

When a child tells you that you are like a parent, it is like a parent telling you that you are being sensible – the last thing in the world that you want to be.

'Fine,' I said. 'If you don't want my help, I won't give it.'

Dodi wants me to go out with Tom.

It started when we were standing in line outside the science block, waiting for class to start. Colin isn't in our group for science, so it was just me and Tom standing with Dodi and Jake, trying not to listen to their conversation.

'What do you want to do this weekend?' Jake asked Dodi.

Dodi tossed her hair over her shoulder and sighed 'I don't know, anything,' and why didn't we all go to the cinema. Sometimes I think the only reason she keeps her hair that long is so she can toss it when she's annoyed, but Jake totally failed to read the signals.

'Poodle,' he murmured. 'I was thinking just me and you.'

Behind their backs, Tom made a puking gesture. I giggled.

Dodi spun round and glared at us. 'What's so funny?' she asked.

'I made a joke,' Tom explained. 'Blue thinks I'm hilarious. Don't you, Blue?'

'Hilarious,' I choked, and Tom patted my hand approvingly.

Later, on our way out of lunch, she held me back from the others.

'He totally likes you,' she said. 'And he's totally cute, if you ignore the spots.'

'I don't think he does like me,' I said.

'If you go out with Tom,' Dodi ploughed on, 'we can go on double dates. We'd be like, two couples. That way I don't have to be alone with Jake.'

I do wonder about Dodi sometimes.

'Why don't you just finish with him instead?' I suggested, but Dodi said she didn't want to hurt his feelings.

'The trouble is,' I said, 'I don't like Tom.'

Dodi said, 'If you loved me, that wouldn't matter.'

I said, 'I do love you, I just don't love Tom.'

Dodi said, mysteriously, 'Well, we will see about that!'

The thing about Dodi is, she never gives up. In English, she made everyone switch places so I was 'accidentally' sitting next to Tom. At afternoon break, she made him share his Snickers with me, all, 'They're Blue's absolute favourite too, aren't they Blue?'

She wanted us all to go to the park together after school. 'Let's skateboard!' she said, and 'You can borrow Tom's!' when I said that, unlike the boys,

I don't take a skateboard with me everywhere I go.

'I don't mean to be rude,' Tom said, 'but I don't lend my wheels to anybody.'

'What, even Blue?'

'I have extra Maths homework,' I said, and ran away before she could suggest a giant group maths study session.

Twig was in the kitchen when I got home, cooking pasta.

'Is it dinner already?' I asked.

'This is tea,' he said.

'Twig has decided to join the after-school rugby club,' Pixie explained.

'Rugby? Twig?' I stared at him, astonished. 'What about, I don't know . . . Science Club?'

'Please!' Twig cried. 'I already know most of the stuff they talk about in Science Club, and they're not even allowed to do experiments. Rugby's excellent. You get to play matches and go on tour and the team are like instant friends. But I have to bulk up, because I'm so skinny compared to all the others.'

Pixie handed him a banana. 'Chop that into it,' she advised.

'A *banana*? In *pasta*?'

'Why not?'

'It just looks disgusting.' I peered into the pan. 'You know there are other ways to make friends, right?'

Twig started grating cheese onto the banana and said I understood nothing.

I made tea and took it out to the garden, where Jas was lying on her front in the grass in pink and orange stripy tights and a knee-length lime green jumper, writing in a notebook while Pumpkin rolled about kneading chewed-up rusk into the grass.

'What are you doing?' I asked.

'Private.'

'Is it your performance piece for the art show?'

'Haven't started that yet.'

'Are you going to do it?'

'I am very, very busy,' Jas said, 'so please could you stop talking to me?'

I lay down beside Pumpkin, who gurgled and shoved a fistful of rusk in my mouth, laughing like a demon. I put him in the middle of the blanket and took my mug to the back of the garden, where I could still watch him without getting covered in food.

Today is that sort of September day when the air feels fresh and damp even though the sun is shining, and there is a big blowy wind stirring up smells of earth and leaves, and the light is all rich and gold. My phone pinged. It was Dodi, with a picture of Tom on his skateboard. 'Forget Maths ☺ Come and join us!'

Very softly, almost like I didn't want Dodi to see me do it, I deleted the photograph. Then I lay back on the bench to watch big fluffy white clouds scud across the pale blue sky.

Thursday 23 September

Flora Skyped, asking could we post her bunny rabbit onesie and also more thermal underwear, because the house is in a dip by a river, dripping with damp and completely unheated.

'I did tell you,' Mum murmured, but Flora was too busy issuing orders to respond.

'I also need new wellies. My old ones got full of water from lying in the stream in my nightie, and they won't dry, and now I think there are things growing in them.'

Twig asked, why was she lying in the stream? Flora said because they had to spend the whole day pretending to be a character from a play, and she was Ophelia, who is a girl in Shakespeare who went mad and drowned herself. Mum said no wonder she was cold and next time maybe she could choose a character less prone to hurling herself into icy waters. Flora said please could Mum just send the clothes, because she was soon going to run out of layers.

'Look what I'm wearing!' she said, and waved her laptop about so we could see her thermal leggings, leg-warmers, boots, mittens and an enormous man's sweater.

Then Mum said did Flora realise how expensive it was to keep sending clothes to Scotland? Flora said fine, if you want me to *freeze to death*, and turned away from the camera.

'Are those *wings* on your back?' I asked.

Flora cried, 'Why are you all so obsessed with how I look?' and logged off.

'They *were* wings,' I said. 'But why?'

'To make her happy,' Pixie said. 'Maybe she's feeling sad.'

Twig asked, 'How does that actually work? The happy thing, I mean?'

Pixie thought quite carefully before she answered. 'It's about showing you won't let the world get to you,' she said. 'Like you're saying, you can try and bring me down, but I don't care because I've got wings to elevate me.'

Twig told her she was barking mad, but affectionately, like he's actually quite fond of her.

'Or, if you're Flora, you could just be making an empty fashion statement,' I suggested.

Pixie said, 'There's no such thing as an empty fashion statement.' Jas said she knew exactly what Pixie meant. 'Clothes should show the world what you are like on the inside,' Pixie said. 'Like you, Jas. So full of colour.'

The two of them beamed at each other, like they were both in a secret colourful dressing club, and I came upstairs to look at my clothes.

Today I am wearing my big grey sweatshirt again, over skinny black jeans and black and white trainers. My hair is in its usual plaits and the only makeup I'm wearing is a little bit of blue mascara which you can't see anyway because of my glasses. Even though inside I am bursting with ideas, I am completely devoid of colour.

Friday 24 September

There was a new picture today.

It was on the corner of Chatsworth Square and the Avenue, and even though Jas made us leave uncharacteristically early this morning, by the time we reached it there was already a crowd of people gathered in a semi-circle in front of it, all laughing.

On the pavement, in the middle of the semi-circle, was a neat pile of dog poo. And on the wall, right above the poo, was a drawing of a life-size black and tan miniature dachshund squatting, seen from the back but looking over his shoulder with an expression that was partly apologetic but also defiant.

'That's hilarious.' Twig had rugby practice before school today (another reason we left early), and was jumping up and down in his kit, trying to keep warm in his shorts, but laughing like everybody else. Only Jas carried on looking serious.

It was strange, looking at the picture. Partly because it was so realistic – I mean because dogs, unlike a field of bluebells or a zebra, do actually exist on London streets. But partly also because lots of other people were looking at it, and it didn't feel so personal, and also – I felt a pang of disappointment – partly because this picture had nothing to do with me. I realised how much I had liked that, the feeling they'd given me when I looked at them – as if the artist was seeing straight through all the layers, straight to what I am like underneath.

Still, I have films of the other drawings. I took my camera out of my bag.

'Please don't make a film,' Jas begged. 'There isn't time.'

'Just a few pictures then,' I said, but she was already walking away. I photographed the dog from different angles to look at later, and ran to catch up with her.

When we arrived at school, Twig asked if he could show my pictures to the boys at rugby practice.

'Please, Blue,' he said when I refused. 'It'll make them laugh. They'll think it's hilarious.'

Twig *knows* I don't like showing my camera to anyone. What I do ... it's not like the chalk artist's drawings. It's not *art*. But Twig was begging me, and looking at him I saw how true it is, when he says how skinny he looks compared to the rest of the boys on the team, and also just how *wrong* too, with his floppy hair and his glasses and his shorts flapping about his legs and his shirt hanging off his bony shoulders ...

'Only the dog pictures,' I said, as I gave him the camera. 'Don't show them anything else.'

The rugby boys did think it was hilarious.

They crowded round the camera, sniggering and pointing and saying things like 'mental' and 'sick' and high fiving Twig when they'd finished looking. I swear Twig seemed to grow about a foot right in front of me.

Then Dodi arrived with Tom and Jake, and even though she also knows how much I hate people looking at my camera, she plucked it out of Twig's hands and started showing Tom my pictures.

Tom laughed and said, 'Excellent! The dog you were telling us about on the first day,' and I thought Dodi was going to faint, she looked so pleased.

'He remembered!' she whispered, when I finally got my camera back and we were walking across the schoolyard towards Spanish. 'He remembered the dog! Even *I* didn't remember the dog, and I was there! Blue, he *so* likes you.'

'He likes me because he remembers I once told a story about a dog trying to do a poo?'

'Oh my God!' Dodi cried, and stopped dead in her tracks. 'What if he is the artist?'

'*Tom?*'

'He does Art! And remember how in Year Nine he and Jake and Colin decorated their skateboards all over with drawings of rats?'

'That doesn't mean . . .'

'It totally *does* mean. He knows you like art. He's sending you secret messages. Look, he's over there!'

She waved manically towards where Tom stood, on the other side of the yard. He waved cheerfully back.

'This is going to be *great*,' Dodi sighed.

When I walked past the dog drawing on my way home, other people had started to scribble comments on the wall above it, things like, 'Who left this lying around?' and, 'Scoop my poop', and lots of much ruder things about dogs and messy pavements. It didn't rain this afternoon, but it drizzled. The chalk – drawing and writing – was fuzzy round the edges, and the dog was starting to look a bit sad.

I have looked and looked at my pictures, but there isn't a bluebell or anything else to link the picture to me.

Could Tom have done this?

The poor dachshund – it looked so dignified. If I'd had a piece of chalk, I'd have written on the wall too. I would have said 'Hey, leave me alone! I'm just doing my thing!'

If people did look on the outside like they do within, then there would be somebody wandering about our neighbourhood with flowers in their hair and chalk dust all over their multi-coloured clothes, and everyone would know without the slightest doubt that this was an artist. But I have not seen a single person who looks like that, except perhaps for mad Mrs Bird who lives underneath the railway arches and ties rags and scarves and plastic bags to the shopping trolley she keeps all her things in. And maybe that does make her an artist in a way, but I don't think she is *my* artist. I think she is just trying to make her life a bit more pretty, which is sort of the same thing but not exactly.

Sunday 26 September

I woke up this morning feeling like someone was watching me, and when I opened my eyes, Jas was sitting on the floor by my bed with her face right next to mine.

'Wake up wake up wake up,' she whispered.

'Go away,' I groaned.

'You have to take me shopping.'

I looked at my phone. 'It's half-past ten. It's Sunday. The shops won't be open yet.'

'They will be by the time we get there.'

I slumped back against my pillow. Jas ran away and came back with a cup of milky warm water with a tea bag floating in it. She watched anxiously as I drank it.

'Is it nice?'

'It's much better than it looks.'

'Can we go now?'

'Can't you go on your own?'

'Apparently I'm too little.' Jas glared in the general direction of Mum's room. 'It's not fair. Twig's staying over with his new rugby friends and you'll probably go off and see Dodi, but I'm not allowed to do a thing on my own. Please, Blue. Please please please please please.'

'All right,' I sighed. I swung my feet out from under the duvet. 'All my friends sleep till at least twelve,' I informed Jas, but that turned out not to be true, because Dodi rang as we turned into Blenheim Avenue.

'Jake just called,' she said. 'He wants to meet up. But it's Sunday morning! Who meets their boyfriend on Sunday morning? I told him I have to hang out with you. I said you're depressed because you're in love with Tom.'

'What?'

'I'm coming over right now.'

'I'm not at home. I'm out with Jas. We're going to . . .' I raised my eyebrows at Jas.

'The toy shop,' she said, and my heart skipped a beat. And I know when I told Dodi, she was thinking the same thing as me, because she was silent for a moment.

'Right,' she said at last. 'I'll see you there.'

The thing about the toy shop is Iris, and her obsession with Sylvanian Families. An obsession so huge her collection used to cover most of the floor of our bedroom and all of the shelf-space as well.

'There's no room for my books,' I used to complain, and, 'They're creepy,' Dodi told her. 'They're miniature toy animals in human clothes.'

Iris didn't care. Every month, when she got her pocket money, she used to march us down to the shop to buy more Sylvanians. After she died, they were the last thing Mum packed away. And until today, Dodi and I never set foot in that shop again.

Jas is too young to remember all that. And this morning – well, by the time I found out where we were going, we were already halfway there.

The shop hasn't changed, but it's smaller than I remembered. The Sylvanians, which used to be at my nose height, were somewhere around my belly button. I crouched down to look at them.

'Hello,' I said. A mother squirrel in a flowery

apron stared back at me, her baby squirrel in her arms. My eyes started to prickle.

'Creepy.' Dodi was standing behind me, her nose all wrinkled like it goes when she's trying not to cry.

'Hideous,' I agreed. We stood there for a while sniffing and looking at those stupid squirrels, then Dodi grabbed something from the rack beside her.

'Look!' It was a bowler hat, the fancy-dress kind that comes with round glasses and a pink nose and plastic moustache attached. She settled the glasses on her nose and smoothed her hand over her upper lip.

'The name's Bond,' she said in a deep voice.

'How is *that* Bond?' I cried, but I couldn't help laughing. That's the thing about Dodi. Walking over, I was so cross with her because of what she said about Tom, but then she knows exactly how to make things better.

'I'm going to get one for all of us for Halloween,' she said. 'I babysat my nephew last night, so I've got loads of money.'

'Found them!' Jas cried, and we turned away from the squirrels and mice and hedgehogs and other woodland creatures and forgot all about Iris and Halloween and James Bond and bowler hats. Because there, surrounded by princess costumes and clown wigs and witches' brooms and animal masks, stood my little sister wearing the most extravagant pair of fairy wings I have ever seen.

Pixie and Flora's wings are like an old pair of jeans next to a couture ball gown compared to Jas's. Pixie and Flora's wings are the sort we used to have in our dressing-up box, white and gauzy with silver edges, four oval hoops like a child's drawing of a butterfly. The wings Jas found today in the toy shop were emerald green with bright blue edging, gold sequins sewn into the top where they peeped up over her shoulders, and gold ribbons trailing down to her knees.

'They're perfect,' Jas declared.

She paid for them with her birthday money, and says she's going to wear the wings to school tomorrow.

'I don't think it's a very good idea,' Mum said when Jas told her.

'Everyone is wearing wings,' Jas said. 'Look at Pixie. Look at Flora.'

'Flora's Flora,' Dodi said. 'And Pixie is Pixie. And they are both mildly insane. No offence, Pixie.'

'None taken,' Pixie replied.

But Jas stuck her chin out and made us all look at Flora's Facebook. There were about a dozen people from her course all dressed in black and pretending they were flying with silver wings on their back just like hers.

'They can't *all* be mad,' Jas said.

'But why do they do it?' Mum was astonished.

'To make them happy,' Pixie said, and Mum looked even more baffled.

'School won't let you,' Twig said.

But the Clarendon Free School dress code is as vague for primary as it is for secondary. We checked their website. 'No bare midriffs,' I read out. 'No short skirts, no swimwear, no high heels.'

'Absolutely nothing about wings,' Jas said.

'Please do not let a single one of my friends see you,' Twig fretted. 'And if they do, deny you are my sister, or they'll all laugh at me.'

Jas said that was Twig's problem, not hers.

I have been reading back through my diary, and I realise I can't remember when I last saw Jas look happy or smile, but I am not sure what to say to help.

'Can't you talk to her?' I messaged Skye. Jas loves Skye, because he taught her to ride without a saddle last summer, and she loves horses almost as much as he does.

'Why?' he replied.

'I just don't like it,' I said. 'She's not doing this because she thinks the wings are pretty. She's making a point, but I don't know what it is, and I can't help feeling that wearing turquoise and emerald knee-length wings is not going to help. Please talk to her. She won't listen to me. She thinks I sound like Mum.'

'Jas won't listen to anybody,' Skye replied. 'And anyway, you can't help people if they don't want you to. That's what my dad always says – people have to learn from their own mistakes.'

'But she's so little!' I wrote.

Skye replied that she might be little, but she was tougher than she looked, and to stop worrying so much.

The Film Diaries of Bluebell Gadsby

Scene Three
Primary Playground,
With Wings

Daytime, 3.30 in the afternoon, outside
the gates of Clarendon Free Primary
School, a four-storey Victorian red
brick townhouse, with white trim
windows, a shrubby garden at the front
and a mini playground at the back.
Sound of multiple recorders from an
after-school music club comes through
open window, together with cries from
a harassed music teacher crying 'No,
no, no, that is not it at all!'

CAMERAMAN (BLUEBELL) and DODI stand
with a gaggle of carers, mothers and a
few fathers as primary school children
of all sizes pour out. On this dry

and mild afternoon, coats are dragged along the ground, gathering dust. Lunchboxes swing. Two small boys stop and hold up the exodus to argue over trading cards.

The crowd parts and flows around them like the Red Sea in that Bible story. A large plimsolled woman with a dachshund on a lead (the presumed star of the last chalk drawing) eyes Cameraman with suspicion before approaching her. She is Mrs Doriot-Buffet, the American neighbour from Chatsworth Square.

MRS DORIOT-BUFFET
Young lady, you should not be filming here without permission.

DODI
She's waiting for her sister. It's for a school project.

CAMERAMAN
I promise to erase it as soon as I get home.

MRS DORIOT-BUFFET

If it's for a school project, why are
you going to erase it?

The exodus has thinned to a few
stragglers, the sort with undone
satchels spewing out worksheets and
half-eaten sandwiches, or scuffed-up
trainers and belligerent attitudes
emerging from their five-minute end-
of-day detentions.

There is still no sign of JASMINE.

MRS DORIOT-BUFFET
(not going away)

I know you. You're those girls
from the square who destroyed Mrs
Henderson's hydrangeas.

DODI
(displaying amazing lack of tact,
even for her)

And you're the fat lady in the
turquoise tracksuit!

A couple of parents nearby snigger. Mrs Doriot-Buffet splutters. Cameraman hands camera to Dodi.

CAMERAMAN
I'd better go and look for her.

DODI
I'll come with you.

Mrs Doriot-Buffet retrieves her child and moves away. Bluebell crosses the playground followed by Dodi, who randomly films everything she passes.

At the far end of the tarmac play area is a door, leading on to a corridor which goes straight on to the office or right towards the toilets. As Bluebell sets off towards the office, four girls emerge from the toilets, giggling and flapping their arms like wings.

Bluebell changes direction.

DODI
(follows, still filming)
Seriously, the toilets?

BLUEBELL
Shhh!

From the far cubicle comes the sound
of muffled crying. Bluebell crouches
down. Through the gap in the door, she
spots a pair of silver high-tops.

BLUEBELL
Jas, it's me. Open the door.

The door to the cubicle creaks open
and Jasmine emerges. Her face is red
and puffy from crying. Her nose is
snotty, and her hair bedraggled.
 In her hands, she holds a pair of
beautiful, shiny broken wings.

This morning the giggling started before we reached the school gates but even so, I thought Jas might get away with it.

She was dressed exactly like Flora and her friends, in black leggings and a black jumper, plus her silver shoes, the yellow scarf trimmed with the green pompoms she made herself in craft classes in Year Four, and the wings. She had cut herself a fringe at the end of the weekend too. It makes her big dark eyes look even more huge, and she'd put a tiny smear of glitter on her cheeks.

As we said goodbye at her school gates, she looked like a very strange, waiflike and beautiful fairy, but also quite a nervous one.

'Are you sure you want to do this?' Dodi asked. 'Because so far everyone has laughed at you, and it's not going to get better.'

Jas whispered, 'Yes.'

Twig asked, 'Are you feeling elevated yet?'

'Shut up,' I told him, and then I said to Jas, 'Remember when Flora got dreadlocks and dyed them pink? You're totally as cool as her.'

'Yeah,' Dodi said, like she was trying hard to sound convincing.

'Tell you what,' I suggested. 'We've got study period last thing this afternoon. We'll skip it and come and pick you up, OK? Then I can film you coming out, and we can send the film to Flora.'

Jas squared her shoulders and stepped into the playground, wings a-flutter, without looking back.

Then, this afternoon, we found her crying in the toilets.

'What happened?' I asked, as I picked up the broken wings.

Jas just carried on crying.

'Let's go home,' I said, but she shook her head.

'I don't want Twig to see me.'

'The park, then. It's not raining. I'll buy you a hot chocolate and we can sit somewhere no-one will see us and you can tell us all about it.'

Jas sniffed and stopped crying.

'Jake's in the park,' Dodi objected, but I gave her a look and she shut up.

Jas and Dodi went to sit behind a tree in the walled garden where nobody ever goes. Dodi and I pooled all the money we had – she still had some from babysitting – and I bought Jas a hot chocolate the way she likes it with baby marshmallows on top, in a paper cup decorated with mini cupcakes.

'This'll help,' I said as I handed it to her, but she started to cry again. 'What?' I asked. 'It's chocolate!'

'The cupcakes!' she wailed, and the whole sorry story came out.

Jas has never had close friends at school. Until this year she always had Twig, and if he's not around she has always been happy to 'just play with whoever' – that's what she said in the park. 'And there were lots of *whoevers*,' she sniffed. 'Everyone was nice, sort of. Until this year.'

Dodi asked, 'What happened this year?', and Jas said it wasn't *what* happened, it was *who*, and *who* were four girls called Megan, Courtney, Chandra and Fran.

'The four girls who were in the playground?' I asked.

'They're called the Cupcake Crew,' Jas said.

Dodi snorted. I shot her another look. She changed the snort into a sort of sniffle.

'They all wear the same cupcake necklace,' Jas explained. 'They spent all summer together and now they're best friends, and everyone's scared of them.'

'But what have they done to you?' I asked.

Jas said they laughed at her.

'Because of the wings?'

'Ever since the first day. They say I dress like a freak.'

'What were you wearing on the first day?'

'Purple leggings,' Dodi said. 'And her ripped dress, and Flora's lace cardigan, and that multi-coloured ribbon in her hair.'

We were quiet for a bit while we thought about this.

'They say I'm a show-off!' Jas cried. 'Just because when we had to write our stupid "what I did in the summer holidays" essay, I wrote mine as a poem to make it less boring, all about learning to ride bareback in Devon with Skye.'

'So ... ?'

So after several weeks of the cupcake girls laughing at her, making everyone else laugh at her and calling her names like the Bare Bum Rider and the Horsefaced Poet, Jas wrote another poem. This one was about all the embarrassing things Courtney and Megan and Chandra and Fran have ever done. When you've been at school with people since nursery, there are loads of things you'd all rather forget. Like the time Courtney forgot to wear pants in reception and told the whole class she had an itchy bottom. And how Megan once came to school with nits and said she was keeping them as pets. And when Fran let a boy kiss her for 50 pence, and Chandra fell asleep during story time and did a fart so loud the whole class heard.

Jas wrote a poem, and then she typed it up and printed loads of copies and stuck one in everyone's locker. But it backfired, because who else in the entire school actually writes poetry? The Cupcake Crew guessed immediately it was her, and they told everyone to stop talking to her.

'I wish you'd told me,' I said.

Jas said she wanted to, but also that she knew I'd only have told her not to do the poem.

'Well of course she would!' Dodi cried. 'Blue would have come up with a sensible solution. Honestly, Jas! Of all the stupid things to do!'

Jas and I both glared at her, but Dodi didn't seem to notice.

'What about the wings?' she asked.

'Flora says you have to stand up to people who are mean to you,' Jas said defiantly. 'That's what she told me, the day she walked me to school. She said, if people know you're afraid, they pick on you. *Nobody* thinks you're afraid if you go to school with wings on your back.'

We were all quiet again.

'It *is* true,' I admitted.

'All the same,' Dodi said, 'you might want to go more mainstream for a while, Jas.'

Jas glared at her again, then sniffed. 'I wore them all day,' she said, and began to pick marshmallows off the top of her hot chocolate. 'Everyone laughed at first, but at break Todd Baker said I looked nice. Todd comes to school every day wearing a waistcoat and a bow tie. He's the only person who still talks to me.'

'I wonder why,' said Dodi.

Jas licked her fingers. 'Then other people said they liked them too. Tilly and Anjali even asked where they could get some. And the cupcake girls didn't say anything, so I thought it had worked. But at home time, they pushed me into a corner and everyone's so scared of them no-one said anything, and Megan was all come on, let's see if you can fly, and they made me run and flap my arms and people were laughing so I hid in the toilets and I tore my wings up myself, even though it was all my birthday money...'

She gulped, and a marshmallow got stuck in her throat.

I thumped her on the back. 'Don't worry,' I said. 'Everything will be better now.'

I don't think I sounded very convincing.

Wednesday 29 September

I tried to call Flora last night. I figured she ought to know Jas stood up to the Cupcake Crew like she advised but that it hadn't worked, and I wanted to ask her what we should do next. But her phone went straight to voicemail, and later, like around midnight, I got a message from her saying sorry, she couldn't talk because for a whole week they are not allowed to speak to anyone but only express themselves through the medium of movement. 'I'm not even supposed to be writing,' she messaged.

Jas's solution for dealing with yesterday's humiliation is to not go to school. This morning she managed to have a temperature of 38.5 degrees, and Mum said she should stay home with Pixie. Twig, who has a bruise under his left eye and a limp in his right leg from rugby practice, said he wanted to stay too.

Jas said, 'You're not ill.'

Twig said, 'Are you?'

'Jas has a temperature,' Mum said.

'Has she?' Twig cried. 'Has she really?'

'Yes,' Jas croaked, glaring at him. 'She has.'

'She's faking,' Twig grumbled as we left the house (early, again, because of his leg and not being able to walk fast). 'She did that thing Flora always used to do, where she drinks tea before putting the thermometer in her mouth. *I* am in actual physical pain.'

'Stop playing rugby then,' I said. 'Do you even like it?'

Twig said that wasn't the point, and he couldn't give up now because that would mean he was weak, and being on the rugby team was a very big deal.

'Your eye is *purple*,' I told him.

Twig said, 'Exactly, it means I'm really one of the team.'

Boys are mad.

'It probably is a good thing for Jas not to go to school for a bit though,' I said, without thinking. Twig asked why, and I had to say 'Oh, nothing,' because yesterday on our way home Jas begged me not to breathe a word to Twig of what had happened.

'Because he warned me,' she said. 'And I don't want him to be right.'

'You have to tell him the truth,' I told her. 'And Mum. Mum can talk to your teachers. She can stop these girls.'

'She'll make a fuss,' Jas said. 'And that'll make things worse.'

I said that I sympathised, but also that sometimes you need help from other people.

'If you tell either of them,' Jas said, 'I will never speak to you again.'

'But ...'

'No.'

So now, as well as not being able to talk to Flora, I am lying to everybody.

*

Today in English Marek Valenta astonished us all.

Miss Foundry announced that we were going to spend the entire period reading aloud from *Of Mice and Men*.

'So we can get a feel for the dramatic, claustrophobic quality of the narrative,' she explained.

I don't know if she genuinely doesn't notice when people look blank, or if she just chooses to ignore us.

'Let's start at the front!' she trilled. 'Marek Valenta, please begin!'

And Marek read.

Most people mumble when they read out loud. A few, like Hattie, speak clearly. Every now and then, someone like Charlie Obuku, who is into drama and wants to be an actor like Flora, hams it up. But no-one ever reads like Marek did today.

Sure, we'd have a little house an' a room to ourself. Little fat iron stove, an' in the winter we'd keep a fire goin' in it . . .

People giggled. Dodi raised her eyebrows. Tom, Jake and Colin stared at him with their mouths open. Cressida and Jodi nudged each other. Marek didn't notice. On and on he read, way beyond the end of the passage Miss Foundry had asked for, and I swear it was like listening to someone in a theatre or on the TV or radio or something, even with his slight Czech accent.

Marek, who to this day has still barely addressed a word to anybody.

'Thank you, Marek.' Miss Foundry was practically crying.

He stopped. He looked dazed. 'Sorry,' he said. 'I just like that part.'

It could have gone either way. The moment when the weird foreign kid held up his hand and confessed to a love of miserable American literature, it could have been the kiss of social death. But like I said, we were astonished. He was so good maybe because he was just doing it for himself, and not trying to convince us the book was a masterpiece. And it was clear he was telling the truth. He wasn't trying to show off – he really did like that part.

Tom started to clap first. Then little by little, the rest of the class joined in, until everyone was cheering and making as much noise as possible, and Marek Valenta was beetroot red with embarrassment and mortification, but also trying quite hard not to grin.

I think, underneath his poker face exterior, Marek Valenta is not as stiff and boring as he likes to pretend.

I think Marek Valenta might even be quite interesting.

The Film Diaries of Bluebell Gadsby

Scene Four
A Strange Boy
in the Park

Afternoon, the park. Watery blue sky. Hazy sunlight. Children running round the adventure playground, café garden full of toddlers and their carers, a huddle of teens in uniform smoking and thinking no-one can see them, a raucous match on the basketball court, dogs tearing about. Everyone making the most of the fine weather as the last leaves on the trees turn red and gold.

In the skateboard park, TOM and COLIN practise tricks called things like Butter Flips and 50/50s and Pogos. They cruise, they flick, they flip, they fall, they get back up again. Every time they pass each other, they slap their hands together in exuberant high fives.

JAKE and DODI sit on a bench, skateboards at their feet. He holds her hand and whispers in her ear. She looks longingly at Colin and Tom (Dodi is an ace skateboarder). CAMERAMAN perches on the back of a separated bench. She is attempting to make a film about skateboarding, trying to remember what Zoran said about the point of art being to make people look at things differently.

As far as she can tell, Colin and Tom look exactly the same on her film as they do in real life. But the camera is also a useful tactic for ignoring Dodi, who is still trying to match-make her with Tom.

TOM
Hey, Blue! Watch this!

He skates to the top of the ramp, twists, falls, smacks his head and lies still. Colin hops off his board and runs over to him. Cameraman carries on filming. Dodi calls out meaningfully.

                    DODI
    Blue, aren't you going to help him?

                  CAMERAMAN
                  He's OK.

                    TOM
          (sits up, rubs his head)
    That was AWESOME. I can see stars.

                    DODI
    Blue, sit with him. He's obviously
              hallucinating.

Tom stands, staggers, sighs, tucks his board under his arm and walks across to Cameraman's bench.

TOM

It does actually hurt.

CAMERAMAN

(heartless)

Serves you right for showing off.

Tom laughs. They sit in amiable silence watching as Dodi, blonde hair flying, takes her turn on the ramp. Cameraman gives up trying to make this film into anything artistic and turns towards the park.

Toddlers, smokers, dogs . . .

Picture freezes beneath the big horse-chestnut tree where a boy stands, alone, leaning against the trunk.

A boy with a pale face floating beneath perfectly coiffed hair, his hands deep in the pockets of an exquisitely tailored leather jacket.

Now Tom sees him too. He waves. Slowly, hesitantly, Marek Valenta waves back.

Dodi skated over as Tom and I watched Marek disappear, and said Jake's parents have invited her for dinner on Saturday, and she thought we should all go.

'But they're not invited,' Jake objected.

Colin said he had a family party. Tom said he'd rather eat his skateboard, and anyway he was going to Bristol tomorrow to see his dad for the weekend. Dodi looked disappointed. I left before she actually suggested I go to Bristol with Tom.

I looked for Marek as I crossed the park, but I didn't see him.

At home, Twig was ordering Jas to explain why she had missed yet another day of school, and Jas was still refusing to tell him.

'I'm sick,' she growled.

'You're lying!'

Pixie, who was mashing hardboiled eggs and avocado for Pumpkin's tea, murmured something about lying being bad for people's karma.

'If you lie,' she said, 'bad things will happen to you in a future life.'

'Bad things will happen to her now if she doesn't tell me the truth,' Twig said. 'Blue knows what's going on, don't you Blue?'

'No,' I said.

'LIAR!'

Pixie cried, 'Karma, karma, karma!' Pumpkin, encouraged by all the shouting, started hurling avocado egg around the kitchen. Twig folded his arms and glared at everybody, looking quite scary because his purple eye is turning green and yellow and he can't really open it.

'All right, I'll tell you!' Jas grumbled.

Afterwards, Twig said hadn't he told her the whole wearing wings to school thing was a terrible idea, and what was she thinking putting those stupid leaflets in people's lockers and she was even more of an idiot than he thought she was. Jas burst into tears.

'I knew something was up!' he shouted. 'I knew it! Why didn't you tell me? I would have sorted them out!'

'Tell him, Blue,' Jas sniffed.

'She didn't want a fuss,' I said. 'She thought it would make things worse.'

Twig started to punch his left hand with his right fist, which I think is something people do before rugby matches, and announced that he was going to kill Courtney and Megan and Chandra and Fran. Pixie murmured that violence was never a solution. Twig said sometimes it was. Jas said she would rather

Twig didn't kill them, but that it was nice of him to offer. She stopped crying. They went outside to practise his catching (which is still hopeless), and I went up to my room and lay on my bed and thought about Marek, standing watching us from under the horse-chestnut tree.

'*Do you miss Prague, Marek?*' I remembered Mum asking when he came for that drink.

'*Yes, I do. Very much,*' he had answered.

I wonder what it is like to leave your country and come somewhere that is completely new? His English is so good, sometimes I forget that he doesn't come from here.

Did he have friends in Prague? When he waved at us, should I have gone over to talk to him?

Sometimes, like when he helped me in English or when he almost smiles at something, I think he likes me, but most of the time he looks at me like I am just weird.

Anyway, I couldn't have spoken to him in the park. He was gone the minute I saw him.

If he'd wanted to talk to us, he would have hung around.

But maybe I should have tried harder, just the same.

I went for a walk with Zoran today, and he said that Gloria is going to Grandma's tomorrow to start getting things ready for the horses.

'There is a lot to organise,' he said. 'Moving twelve horses across the country ... will you help?'

'What, *ride to Devon*?'

Zoran laughed and said that charming though it was picturing the entire Gadsby family setting off on a giant pony trek from London to Dartmoor, the horses would actually be going by truck.

'I meant, will you help us pack up in London, and unpack in Devon? Blue, what are you doing?'

'Hmm?'

'You keep staring at the pavement.'

With everything that has been happening with Jas, I haven't thought about the drawings for a while, but it has become a habit, I guess. Gutters, alleys, walls – everywhere I go, I am looking for them.

'No reason,' I said. 'Of course we'll help.'

After Iris died, when our whole family was falling apart from being so sad, Zoran is the one who saved us. I'm not exaggerating. We had become these crushed, sad little people, but then he came to live with us, and even though he is quite chaotic and not always very efficient, he managed to make us all feel better. I'm very happy that he's going to live with Grandma, but I don't like the idea of him going away. Not just because, along with Skye and Grandma, he is the only person who ever listens to me, but also because the way things feel at home right now, I think we need him here.

'Jas is being bullied at school,' I told him, and explained about the Cupcake Crew (I left out the bit about Jas's poems and the wings).

'Do your parents know?' he asked.

'She doesn't want them to. Zoran, what should I do?'

'She won't let you get involved?'

'She doesn't think I can help.'

Zoran frowned as he thought. 'I should talk to your parents.'

'Please don't!' I begged.

Zoran said fine, but made me swear that if things got worse, I would call him. Then he said that all I could do was to try to make Jas feel better about herself.

'How?'

'I don't know! Do something fun with her.'

We passed another alleyway, then turned onto the Avenue, just opposite the toy shop. Suddenly I had an idea.

'Can you lend me some money?' I asked.

There was a smell of burning in the house when I got home. I followed it upstairs. Jas was sitting on the floor of her bedroom, holding some old hair straighteners of Flora's in one hand and a strand of smoking hair in the other.

'Do you know how to use these?' she demanded.

'What are you *doing*?'

'It's for those girls.' Twig wandered in from the bathroom, examining his greeny-yellow eye in a hand-mirror.

'What girls?' I asked.

'Those cupcake creatures. She's trying to look like them. She's basically giving in.'

'I'm not giving in!' Jas glared at him. 'I'm just following Dodi's advice.'

'What *was* Dodi's advice?' I asked.

'To be more mainstream.'

Twig grunted that Jas couldn't be mainstream if she tried. Jas threw the hair straighteners at him. He dodged. They landed on his desk instead, knocking a glass of water all over his maths homework.

'I bought chalks,' I said.

Twig stopped shouting. Jas frowned.

'Let's draw,' I said.

And that is how we spent our Saturday evening.

We practised with chalk flowers on the paving outside the kitchen, then worked our way up the wall and on to the trellis before moving to the front of the house. Our drawings are nothing like the chalk artist's. Those are art. Ours look like children's scribbling, because the sad truth is none of us are any good at drawing, and we can only do flowers and birds and cats, but when you have lots and lots of them in different colours all squished together higgledy-piggledy, it doesn't matter.

The final effect was like one of those cards where you have a picture of loads of jelly beans or M&Ms so close up you sort of lose sense of what they are, and just see a big jumble of shape and colour. Except more messy. Really, *really* messy. So messy that by the time we had finished, way after it got dark and we could only see what we had done by street light at the front and the garden light at the back, the three of us were covered head to toe in multi-coloured chalk.

'You look like a butterfly,' I told Jas. She'd used mainly pink and orange chalks for her cats, and rubbed her face a lot.

'A butterfly!' she scoffed.

'And Twig looks like a sort of sci-fi warrior,' I said, because his face was all blue and white.

'But your face is clean . . .' Twig exchanged a glance

with Jas. I started to back away but they were already pouncing on me.

I thought about what Pixie said, about clothes showing on the outside what you look like inside. *This is me*, I thought as I put away the chalks. *Messy and colourful and much more crazy than I look.*

After we'd finished, I sat in the bath for ages, watching the water change colour as the chalk washed off me. I wonder what a chalk artist looks like when a drawing is finished. Is it like us, a multi-coloured bird or alien or butterfly? I don't think that's possible, because if someone like that was around surely people would notice. Maybe the opposite is true. Maybe, when the chalk artist draws, all the vivid colour and strange beauty flow right out and into the picture, so that in the end he or she isn't multi-coloured and shining, but rather grey and tired.

I guess Zoran was right. Maybe it won't last, but doing something fun *did* help. But I'd be lying if I said it was the only reason I did it. I want the chalk artist to see what we've done.

I want to see what the next drawing will be.

I pulled the plug. Sunset-coloured water swirled around the drain and disappeared.

Sometimes you only notice things when you see them through other people's eyes. It was like that at lunchtime.

Ever since that English lesson when he read out loud, the boys have become obsessed with Marek Valenta.

'Why?' Dodi said, when they were talking about him at the end of Maths. 'He's just a secret swot, and he clearly doesn't *like* any of us.'

'Does that matter?' Tom asked. '*We* like *him*. He's so odd! Let's ask him to eat with us.'

He bounced over to Marek, and carried on bouncing him all the way to the canteen. I don't think anyone could resist Tom, once he's decided something.

At lunch, the boys asked Marek who his favourite football team was (something Prague) and did he skateboard (he prefers roller-blading). Hattie asked why he loved Steinbeck so much and did he like acting (he just thinks it's a great book, and no). There was an awkward silence, and then Tom changed the subject and asked me what I was doing for half-term.

Dodi beamed. 'Blue's going to Devon,' she said. 'To help Zoran and Gloria move the horses.'

Tom asked, what horses. Dodi explained. 'I can't believe you've never been to Gloria's stables,' she said. 'They're so cool. They're right under the motorway. You should ask Blue to take you.'

I glanced up. Marek was frowning, looking from Dodi to me like he couldn't believe I just let her talk instead of me. He looked away when he saw me looking, but I felt hot with embarrassment.

I hadn't realised until then how much it actually annoys me that Dodi won't let me speak.

'I'm actually allergic to horses,' Tom said. 'Otherwise I'd go like a shot. What's everyone else doing?'

Hattie is going to violin camp. Tom is going back to Bristol, and Colin is going with him. Dodi is repainting her bedroom.

'And I'm helping her,' Jake said.

Tom laughed and called Jake a sentimental idiot. Colin elbowed him in the ribs. Hattie said she wished she had a boyfriend as sweet as him. Jake went red.

Dodi flinched. I saw it, and Marek saw it. His eyes widened again, and that is when I saw something else.

Tom's right – Jake *is* sentimental. But Hattie's right too, he's also sweet. And I love Dodi, but she shouldn't try to make me do things I don't want, or treat Jake the way she does.

I don't know if the chalk artist saw our pictures, but it's too late now. It rained last night, and all our drawings have disappeared. Jas's good mood, however, has lasted.

'The cupcake girls have asked me to be their friend.'

'Their friend?' Twig looked appalled.

'It's true!'

'When did this happen?' I asked.

Jas said, 'They've apologised. They say they didn't mean to upset me. They were just having a bit of fun. They like my hair. They've promised me a cupcake pendant.'

'Fun?' Twig cried. 'Hair?? CUPCAKES?'

Jas said if Twig didn't shut up, she would use her straighteners on him, and not just to burn his hair.

The Film Diaries of Bluebell Gadsby

Scene Five
The End of an Era

Lunchtime, the stables under the motorway. Twelve huddled horseboxes facing into a tiny yard sandwiched between a leisure centre and a bus depot. A big plane tree by the entrance to a narrow passage, just wide enough for a horse and rider, leading to a sawdust ring beneath a network of busy roads. In the riding ring, non-broken cones sit in an orange circle beside striped jumping poles and cross-shaped supports.

The doors to the box at the back of the yard are open. Crates of stuff are piled up inside. Halters and leather wax, horse brushes and combs, hoof picks and saddle pads. There is a pile of saddles, a crate full of bridles, another for girths and stirrups, each labelled for an individual pony or horse, crates with tags saying 'medication', 'whips', 'boots', 'hats'.

Outside in the yard is a growing pile of junk. Broken saddles, chairs, electric heaters, traffic cones, bits of rope, a burst football, torn waterproofs, an old mattress. The range is astonishing.

CAMERAMAN (BLUEBELL) crosses the yard, into the tiny office and up the rickety stairs to the flat above. More boxes, full of china, cutlery, books, bed linen. Suitcases bulging with clothes, pictures stacked on the floor, grimy outlines on the walls where they used to hang. Furniture labelled with different coloured stickers – green for the few items going to Devon, orange for everything that is to be sold or given away.

Back in the yard, ZORAN, GLORIA, TWIG and MOTHER sit on benches eating crisps with cheese and pickle sandwiches and drinking mugs of sweet, strong tea. JASMINE eats standing up, half-hidden by the open top half of a stable door. A pony (Mopsy, her old favourite) hangs its head over the door. She nudges Jas, who offers her a piece of sandwich. Mopsy signals her dislike of pickle by blowing air noisily through her nostrils. Pony snot lands on Jasmine's brand new sky blue hoody. She squeals and pushes Mopsy away.

JASMINE
My new top! It's all dirty!

MOTHER
I did tell you not to wear it.

JASMINE
I had to! What if someone had seen me?

MOTHER
What could it possibly matter?

JASMINE
(tossing her newly straightened,
super-swishy hair and sounding
remarkably like Flora)
You wouldn't understand.

Jas has changed now that she is friends with the Cupcake Crew.

Ever since Gloria came back from Devon on Monday, Twig and I have been at the stables every day after school to help her pack, but today was the first time Jas came, even though out of all of us Jas is the one who loves Gloria the most. Being friends with Megan, Courtney, Chandra and Fran means being exactly like them, and hanging out with dirty animals isn't one of the things they do.

It started with the hair straighteners. Then, the day after our chalk drawing, there was the shopping expedition with Mum. Now, as well as the right hair, she has the right pastel hoodies from the right shop, the right trainers and the right jeans.

We watched as Jas, well out of Mopsy's reach, rubbed away at her sweatshirt, still trying to clean it. Mopsy, who is the cleverest pony in the yard as well as the smallest, reached over the top of her box, pulled the bolt back neatly with her teeth, pushed open her door, ambled over to Jas and blew down her neck.

Everybody laughed. Mopsy looked round, ears waggling like she was saying 'Aren't I clever?' Jas screamed and pushed her away again.

'Why can't you leave me alone!' she screeched.

Zoran put his arm round Mopsy's neck and pushed her back into the box, remembering to padlock the door. Jas flounced away to clean her sweatshirt in the bathroom upstairs.

'If you have to change who you are in order to be friends with someone,' Gloria observed, 'that someone is not a true friend.'

Which is easy to say when you're a grown-up, and a lot more difficult if you have to go to school.

I don't like seeing the stables look like the way they did today, like something that has ended. I told Mum, who said she didn't either but also that nothing new can start without something old ending first, that this was also part of the circle of life and that I should just think how much happier the horses are going to be in Devon.

We were sitting in what used to be the riding ring. I drew a circle in the sand with my finger, and thought about how the chalk artist still hasn't responded. Then I thought that when Mum talked about the circle of life, we were both thinking about Iris, and how difficult it is sometimes for that circle to keep on turning. I told her about wishing Zoran would stay even though I was glad he was going to live with Grandma. Her eyes shone a bit, and I knew she was thinking about the time after Iris too, when he first came to live with us and saved us from being crushed.

'Nothing is more important than for all of us to be happy,' she said, in her fierce I'm-not-crying voice, and pulled me into a hug.

I do love Mum, especially when she listens.

Tuesday 12 October

Flora Skyped. She has a cold. This time she was dressed in a thick fleecy dressing gown, a polo-neck jumper, flannel pyjamas, bed socks, two shawls and a woolly hat, and she kept on blowing her nose.

'That is what comes of floating around rivers in your nightie,' Mum scolded. 'Even if you were wearing wellies.'

Flora said that had nothing to do with it. Pretending to be tragic heroines, Flora said, was the best bit about acting school, and why do people make such a big deal about wearing nightclothes outside?

'It's just like wearing a dress,' she said. 'The reason I got ill has nothing to do with drowning. It's the house, Mum. It's so damp my sheets are actually wet when I go to bed, and there's no heating.'

'I'm sure they're not actually wet,' Mum said. 'Not *dripping*.'

Flora said they were totally dripping and she had to dry them with a hairdryer. 'I'm practically dying,' she said. 'I have to come home right now.'

Mum said, 'But you've only just left!'

'I am sorry,' Flora huffed, 'if the prospect of my imminent return fills you with displeasure.'

Twig said, 'Oh my God, she even *talks* like she's in a play.'

Flora changed tack. 'The thing is,' she said, 'I've got a job.'

'A *job*?'

'A friend wants me to be in his play. It's *Romeo and Juliet*. I'm Juliet.'

Mum said that was wonderful, who was this friend and where was he putting on the play? Flora said his name was Angel, he's done loads of plays already and this one would start in a pub in North London, but that it would definitely get transferred to a proper theatre.

'Definitely?' Mum asked.

'Possibly,' Flora conceded.

'But you're in Scotland,' I pointed out.

Flora said she knew that, and that was why she had decided she was going to leave drama school.

Mum repeated, 'Leave? But you've only just got there!'

'You don't understand!' Flora cried. 'Everything we do here is useless! We have whole classes just teaching us to breathe. Breathe! Yesterday I had to lie on the floor and learn how to massage my tongue.'

Mum said she was sure massaging your tongue was very useful.

'I want to do Angel's play,' Flora said.

Mum said, 'No,' and closed the laptop.

Saturday 16 October

Zoran and Gloria drove to Devon today. The stables and the flat are almost empty. We helped them load the furniture and things Gloria wants to keep into the removals lorry she hired, together with all the horsey things that aren't still needed in London. Earlier in the week, they took all the last things to the dump and charity shops. An auction company took away the things they could sell, like her iron bed-frame and her dad's vintage motorbike, and the council came to take away the fridge and dishwasher and old mattresses. There is nothing left now but the horses themselves, enough feed for a few days, hay nets and brushes and water pails and halters and all the other things horses seem to need. They will be here until Friday with Gloria's friend Penny in charge of the volunteers who will have to exercise them. Skye and his parents are going to help Zoran and Gloria unload when they get to Devon.

It's strange seeing the stables like this. I don't care what Mum says about endings being the start of new beginnings. It was already dusk as Zoran and Gloria drove the truck out of the yard, that sort of early dark damp cold which makes you realise summer is over and isn't coming back for a very, very long time.

I felt sad.

Twig and I sat around for a while after they had gone. We waved them off from the entrance to the yard, and then we petted the ponies we used to ride back in the days when Grandma forced us to have lessons, and then we wandered back through the passageway to the riding ring, and sat on the ground with our backs against the wall.

The ring doesn't even look like it's part of a riding school any more. They've taken up the fence that bordered it and packed that off to Devon too. All that's left is a large rectangle of sawdust with a circular track round the edges made by the ponies, with a wall on one side and a concrete pedestrian area on the other where kids kick balls and hang out on their skateboards, and a motorway overhead, and one brave plane tree reaching up towards the light.

'Zoran says that the people who have bought the stables are going to tear them down to build flats,' I said. 'So there will be nothing to remind people that twelve ponies once lived here. And don't you dare say they'll be happier in Devon. I *know* they'll be happier in Devon. The point is they won't be *here*.'

Twig just stared at the empty yard.

'Do you ever think,' I asked, 'about how much has happened? I mean, I'm only fourteen, and I feel like millions and millions of things have happened to me, so much that I can't imagine there's any more room for new things ever again. And yet here are Zoran and Gloria, who are practically ancient, off to start a brand new life.'

'I miss Jas,' Twig said. 'Do you think Jas will even come to Devon?'

'Of course she will,' I said. 'She loves Devon. And she loves all this, really. She's just distracted right now. Anyway, she has to. She's only ten.'

But when we got home, Jas was marching round the house in a black and white mini-kilt, knee-high socks, a tatty old blazer of Flora's and an old tie of Dad's, with back-combed hair sprayed grey, black lipstick, tonnes of eyeliner, her face plastered in white stage makeup and fake blood dripping down her neck.

'Take a photograph,' she ordered before I was even in the door. 'I have to send the girls a picture of my outfit.'

'Once again,' Mum shouted, appearing behind her with her a wailing Pumpkin on her hip, 'you are *not* going out dressed like that.'

'I'm a zombie schoolgirl,' Jas informed me. 'For Halloween. Tell her.'

'You are a zombie,' Twig agreed. 'But I'm not sure you're a schoolgirl. Not in Year Six, anyway.'

Jas said, what was that supposed to mean? Twig said, what did she think it meant?

'You just look much older than you are,' I said.

'But that's the whole point!' Jas wailed. 'Courtney says Halloween is going to be huge this year. She says we have to have the best costumes, *or else.*'

'Or else what?' Twig asked, but Jas wouldn't say.

'Why is Halloween going to be huge?' I asked.

'Mrs Doriot-Buffet,' Mum sighed. 'It's because she's American. She's been dropping leaflets all round the square, saying we have to decorate.'

'Everyone's going to be here!' Jas cried. 'Everyone! Blue, take the picture!'

I took the picture. Jas emailed it to Courtney. She and Mum argued late into the night about hemlines, makeup and how many shirt buttons Jas was allowed to undo.

Monday 18 October

The chalk artist has responded at last!

Flowers, vines, cats, birds. Today's drawings were all over the pavement outside our house, the same motifs we used when we drew on it, but so much better they made me wish all over again I could be as good on the outside as I am in my head. The artist's roses looked like real flowers had bloomed all over the pavement. The ivy looked like it was growing through the cracks, and the cats looked they were about to pounce on birds that were actually flying. Apart from all that though, they were the same drawings.

Jas crouched down to look at them, tracing one of the cats with her finger. 'It's like a picture book,' she said. 'Like a different world. Like in Mary Poppins.'

Twig scoffed, 'What, you think if you jump into them you'll end up in a magic world?'

'I wish we could,' Jas said. 'I wish Mary Poppins lived with *us*. Pixie's hopeless. All she's done is those wings, and that wasn't any help at all.'

'Jas, are you OK?' I asked.

Jas sighed, stood up and said please could we now go to school. 'I can't be late,' she said. 'We're having a meeting about Halloween.'

'You and the Cupcake Crew?' Twig said.

'Me and my *friends*,' she corrected.

'I'll catch up with you,' I told Twig. 'I just want to take a few pictures.'

Mrs Henderson came out while I was photographing.

'It wasn't us,' I assured her. 'In case you were wondering.'

'I wasn't,' she replied. 'These are far too good.'

'Do you know who it could be?' I asked. She shook her head, regretfully like she wished she *did* know, not so she could tell them off but to say how pretty the drawings were.

Zoran is right. Art does change people.

'I haven't a clue,' she said. 'But it seems to me, after your antics the other day, that whoever did this has been watching you.'

'Do *you* think it's creepy?' I asked.

'In a way,' Mrs Henderson said. 'But it's also rather lovely.'

Dodi made me run out of school as soon as the bell went, to avoid seeing Jake, and said that if he saw us I had to tell him we were doing homework together at my house, but when we came out Jas was waiting for me, sitting on the low wall just outside our gates, all bunched up with her face on her folded arms.

'What's up?' I asked.

She shook her head of perfectly straight, glossy hair and the tip of her nose went red. 'I just wanted to go home with you.'

I glanced at Dodi. She looked back at the playground and said, 'Come on, then, let's go!'

Jas stared at Dodi, then at me, and bit her lip.

'Hurry *up*,' Dodi said.

Maybe it's because Dodi is an only child, but I don't think she understands that sometimes there are things you can say to your own sister that you can't say to, well, your friend's sister.

Jake came out as I tried to explain. 'Let's leave them to it, Poodle,' he said, and she walked away with him, looking back at me like she wanted to kill us all.

One of the school coaches pulled up, full of boys singing rugby songs. The doors opened and Twig appeared, covered in mud with a big slit in his lip that was bleeding. He saw us from the top of the steps and ran over.

'I played my first match!' he said. 'And I scored! Well, I almost scored. I would have if I hadn't dropped the ball. What's up with Jas?'

'I'm guessing it was those cupcake girls,' I said.

'I will kill them,' Twig vowed. I think maybe the blood dripping from his lip was making him a bit mad. 'I'll get the team to help. They're good at hurting people. Look at my lip!'

We walked home, just the three of us. This time it took two cups of tea and a multi-pack of chocolate biscuits for Jas to tell us her story, which is basically that Courtney hates Jas's costume. Or rather, that she hates it on Jas.

'If she wears this,' Courtney had said, like Jas wasn't even there, 'she will look better than us.'

Megan, Courtney, Chandra and Fran had decided to dress up as witches. But after seeing Jas's costume, they decided it would be much better for them to be zombie schoolgirls. So Courtney told Jas to bring the whole costume in tomorrow, including the makeup and Flora's blazer and grey hairspray and Dad's tie, and Jas asked but what about her?

'You can be a witch,' Megan said.

'Not a zombie,' Courtney warned.

'Don't even try it,' Chandra giggled.

'You can't dress like us,' Fran explained. 'Not until

you're *one* of us.'

Jas asked if she would still get the cupcake necklace.

'Seriously?' Twig looked disgusted.

'What did they say?' I asked.

Jas said they just laughed.

She came into my room after her bath this evening, while I was reading a long ranting message from Dodi all about how Jake won't leave her alone about booking the theme park for her birthday, and it was all my fault because if I had been there I could have stopped him. I threw the phone on my bed and shuffled up on my window seat to make room for Jas. In pyjamas, with her long hair still damp from washing and smelling of apple shampoo, you remember Jas is only ten. She pulled the spare blanket off my bed, wrapped it round her shoulders and sat on my window seat in a forlorn little ball. I sat next to her and put my arms round her.

'Devon soon,' I said. 'It'll be better there. You can forget all about those stupid girls.'

She leaned into me and sniffed.

"You will come with us on Thursday to say goodbye to the horses, won't you?' I said, and she nodded.

'Who *is* doing the pictures, Blue?' she asked.

My phone pinged. Dodi again, this time saying should we all get together on Friday before I go to Devon – her, Jake, me and Tom.

Tom. The dachshund drawing. Suddenly, I knew that I really didn't want the chalk artist to be him.

Ping! 'Well? What do you think?'

I don't understand how exactly Dodi thinks I can save her from Jake, but I do know one thing: I don't want to go out with Tom, and I do want Dodi to stop going on about it.

It's my turn to stand up for myself.

Tuesday 19 October

Dodi and Jake have split up, and I think that it's my fault.

'So I told Tom you like him,' she whispered as we filed into English, 'and he wants to talk to you after class.'

'You did what?'

'You're welcome,' she said, and skipped across the room to her desk.

Today Miss Foundry announced that after half-term school will be organising a trip for the whole class to go and see a theatre adaptation of *Of Mice and Men*, and that this would be a wonderful opportunity to see Steinbeck's work brought to life.

'The dramatic tautness of the narrative!' Miss

Foundry cried. 'The tragic irony of fate! Take these forms home for signing and bring them back before the holidays!'

Poor Miss Foundry. She looked so disappointed when no-one reacted to her announcement.

'It will be fun!' she insisted.

'Yay!' I said feebly, feeling sorry for her, and 'Yay!' Tom echoed, presumably feeling sorry for me.

Dodi beamed, watching us.

I have never left a classroom so fast at the end of any lesson. The bell went and I just *bolted*, but Tom came right after me.

'Blue!' he called.

I stopped running. I mean, I didn't want to. I would happily have run straight out of school and all the way home just to avoid having *that conversation* with Tom, but people were starting to pile out of other classrooms and they were blocking my way. Tom caught up with me. I don't think I've ever seen him look so embarrassed.

'The thing is . . .' he paused to clear his throat, and that is when I started to feel properly angry with Dodi and not just annoyed, because I love Tom, I really do, but I also really, *really* don't want to go out with him and it's not fair of her to make him think I like him.

'Listen,' I interrupted, but at the same time another voice said, 'Blue,' and Marek appeared.

'Are you going to go to the play?' he mumbled.

'Probably,' I said.

'Cool.'

That was all. But by the time I looked round again, Tom had gone.

Dodi was so annoyed she didn't talk to me all day.

'I'm sorry.' I was still conciliatory as we put our things away in our lockers. 'I just don't like him.'

I wouldn't have said what I did if Jake hadn't asked. And none of it might have happened at all if Marek or Tom hadn't been there. But Marek and Tom were there, and Jake did ask.

'You do like him,' Dodi said. 'You just won't admit it.'

A few lockers away, Marek was talking to Tom. I remembered how he stared at lunch the other day when Dodi was nagging Tom to come to the stables. How it made me realise that she never listens and is always deciding things for me.

And then I remembered how she called Jas's poem stupid.

And how yesterday, she was more concerned about her and Jake than how my little sister was feeling.

'I'm not asking you to *marry* him,' Dodi grumbled.

'I just think it would be nice. Then we can go on . . .'

'Double dates,' I said. 'You said.'

And I'd just had enough.

'Tom?' I called out.

'Now what are you doing?' Dodi asked.

'Can you come over here?'

Tom bounced over.

'I don't like you,' I told him. 'I'm sorry. I mean, I love you, but not like that. I hope you don't mind.'

'Not in the least,' Tom said. 'I don't like you either. That's what I was trying to tell you at lunchtime.'

Dodi went red. Tom and I both burst out laughing, and once we started we couldn't stop. I could see that people were staring at us and that Dodi was furious, but it only made me laugh more. It was so – so liberating. Like I hadn't realised just how much I hated her going on at me about Tom until now, and how good it felt knowing that it was over.

Jake said, 'Blue doesn't like Tom? But Poodle, why did you say she did?' and we laughed even more.

'Go on,' I hiccoughed. 'Tell him.'

And I think I knew then it was wrong. Because I didn't just feel free, I felt powerful – like I could say whatever I wanted. And I *wanted* to say a lot.

'Tell him,' I repeated, when Dodi stayed silent, 'the real reason why you want me to go out with Tom.'

I can't believe I said that now. I wish I hadn't.

'Poodle?'

Dodi burst into tears and ran away.

Pixie has given Jas a tiara. 'To channel your inner princess,' she told her. 'You could wear it for Halloween.'

'I don't want to be a princess,' Jas said, but she wore the tiara anyway so as not to disappoint Pixie. Flora Skyped later and said how much she liked it.

'Don't you think it's drippy?' Jas asked.

'You're thinking of the wrong princesses,' Flora told her. 'You're thinking of the ones who wear pink and droop about waiting for Prince flipping Charming to come and slay their dragon. *I'm* talking about the sort of princess who wields swords and wears armour and gallops about killing the dragons herself *while* wearing a tiara. Show me.'

Jas jumped on to a chair and started making stabbing, thrusting moves with an imaginary sword. Everyone cheered, even Mum who didn't have a clue what was going on.

She is taking it to school tomorrow.

'Seriously?' Twig said. 'After the wings?'

'I'm not going to wear it,' Jas said. 'I'm just going to *show* it. For Halloween, to see if I can go as a princess.

She wore the tiara all evening, even in the bath, but afterwards when she was drying and straightening her hair, I tried it on too. And there *is* something about tiaras. Something not Barbie but glamorous and powerful and strong. I waved regally at the mirror.

Imagine all the power you would have if you were a queen.

I don't know what you're supposed to do when you've stood up to someone, or been mean to them. It's not something that has ever happened to me before. I waited all evening for Dodi to text me about what happened this afternoon, but tonight my phone has been silent. It was Tom who messaged later, to say that Jake and Dodi had spent ages talking, and that Jake had finished with her. So then *I* texted *her*.

'I'm sorry,' I wrote. 'I didn't mean for that to happen.'

She hasn't answered. Suddenly powerful doesn't feel so good.

The Film Diaries of
Bluebell Gadsby

Scene Six
The Ponies

Lunchtime, the pedestrian area outside
the stables under the motorway, where
six horse trailers have been given
exceptional leave to park and stand
open for loading. Quite a crowd has
assembled. Neighbours, former pupils,
stable-hands, friends. The buyers from
the leisure centre and a man from
the council. Quite a few people are
crying. Toddlers have to be restrained
from running to hug ponies' legs.

GLORIA holds a bunch of flowers
someone has brought her, which MOPSY
is munching without her noticing
while she gives a farewell speech
about how much it has meant to her to
work in such a wonderful place with

such amazing people, and how she will never forget any of them. One of the stable volunteers, a small girl with pigtails, runs away towards the riding ring, overcome with emotion.

GLORIA
(uncharacteristically weepy)
There is something truly magical about a riding school under a motorway. I shall carry you all forever in my heart.

Mopsy sneezes agreement and goes back to chewing a tulip. People laugh. A TWEEDY WOMAN HOLDING BACK A TODDLER hands Gloria a tissue.

TWEEDY WOMAN
The ponies will be happier in the country, dear.

And then Gloria and TWIG and ZORAN and SKYE'S FATHER ISAMBARD and SKYE'S

FATHER ISAMBARD'S FRIEND FROM DEVON
and various stable-hands begin to load
the ponies into the trailers. Some
accept their fate with resignation.
Mopsy, possibly high on his bouquet
of flowers, tries to escape. Gloria
catches him, pushes him into the
trailer and bolts the door. Mopsy
neighs loudly to express disgust.

TWEEDY WOMAN
Attagirl, Gloria! You show 'em!

Final hugs and handshakes are being
distributed when the small volunteer
with pigtails re-emerges, no longer
crying, a look of wonder on her
freckled face.

SMALL VOLUNTEER WITH PIGTAILS
Gloria! Gloria! Have you seen?

GLORIA
Seen what? What are you talking
about?

SMALL VOLUNTEER WITH PIGTAILS
The drawings! The horse drawings! You have to come and look!

And so they go. The former pupils and the neighbours, the manager of the leisure centre and the man from the council, the volunteers and the Gadsby family, and they stand in the sawdust of what used to be a riding ring and they gape and laugh and point and tell each other they can't believe what they are seeing.

Across the wall beneath the motorway, tucked away where no-one would see them unless they went to look, twelve chalk ponies gallop through a grassy meadow.

There are hills and trees, a river. Blue sky with puffy white clouds. It's a rough drawing, not as neatly executed as the zebra or the flowers or the dachshund. It's a lot bigger and looks like it must have been done in a hurry, but even so.

It's obvious, just looking at it. The ponies do look happier in the country.

There wasn't time to think too much about the drawings, because we had to go and fetch Jas.

She didn't come with us to the stables. School broke up for half-term at lunchtime, but when Twig and I raced round to the primary school to collect her, she said she was going to the shopping centre with Courtney, Megan, Chandra and Fran.

'But what about the ponies?' Twig asked.

'Shh!' Jas begged. 'They'll hear you!'

'You're not allowed to go shopping on your own,' I said.

'I won't be on my own, I'll be with them. Please let me! Please?'

'But Jas, with them?' I asked.

She looked so desperate, as Megan and Courtney and Chandra and Fran swished up to us, and they actually seemed so nice, like none of the things she told us about them could ever have happened, and it seemed to matter so much, that I said all right, fine.

'But I'll come and pick you up at the shops.' I pulled her aside to tell her my conditions. 'We can't go home without you, or there'll be a fuss.'

I told her to meet us by the ice-cream place in the shopping centre at three o'clock. We were five minutes late arriving but she wasn't there. I scanned the crowds for her.

'Over there,' said Twig. He pointed. Jas and the four swishy girls were standing in a huddle by the cupcake stand, about twenty metres from us. The four girls were talking. Jas was shaking her head and backing away.

'We have to rescue her!' Twig started running towards them, but I held him back.

'Don't make things worse,' I said.

But now another group was approaching them. Five boys. Four dressed like any other boy, in jeans and T-shirts and trainers and hoodies. One, tiny in comparison, wearing a waistcoat and a bow tie.

'That must be Todd,' I said. 'Remember, she told us about him?'

The cupcake girls nudged each other. Jas took another step away. The tallest girl (Courtney) pulled her back while the dark-haired one (Chandra) snatched her bag and started rooting around inside it. And then everything went very fast.

'A freak for a freak!' Chandra cried, jamming Jas's tiara on her head.

The hoody boys pushed Todd towards Jas. He stumbled. She put her hands out to stop him falling. The girls pushed her closer to him.

'Kiss her! Kiss her! Kiss her!'

As the taunts and laughing grew louder, I thought I saw Jas stand taller. The light glinted off her tiara, and just for a moment she was the princess Flora had talked about – eyes flashing, nostrils flared, off to kill a dragon.

'Shut up!' she snarled. 'Shut up! Shut up! Shut up!'

'What's the matter, Your Majesty?' Courtney crowed. 'Isn't he your boyfriend?'

'We have to help her!' Twig said. We both started to run, but then we stopped again, because Jas was already pulling Todd away. The cupcake girls and the hooded boys all roared with laughter, but Jas marched with her nose in the air, and because she had her back to them they couldn't see how hard she was trying not to cry.

We took them home and fed them cake.

'I thought they wanted to be my friends,' Todd explained as he ate.

'Same,' Jas said. 'I thought they liked me now I dress like them. I wish I'd gone to see the ponies instead. At least I know they love me.'

'I hate looking like everybody else,' Todd said.

'Me too!' Jas cried. 'Oh, me too!'

Todd stayed for supper. He called his mum to tell her where he was, and Pixie spoke to her too, using a very grown-up voice no-one had ever heard before, and he and Jas locked themselves away in her room with a bag of Flora's old makeup, 'To look as unlike ourselves as possible,' Jas announced.

Dad came back from Devon this afternoon – for good, this time. He rang the doorbell three times then flung the door open shouting, 'I'm home!' and then he laughed and laughed when Jas hurled herself down the stairs screeching 'Daddy!'

'Who are you and what have you done with my daughter?' he cried, because Jas was transformed. There was no trace of the sad little girl trying not to cry in the shopping centre. The effect of all that makeup was spectacular – like when we were covered with chalk, but more defined. Jas was luminous in shades of gold eyeshadow, lipstick and bronzer over a pancake thick layer of foundation. Todd was darkly shimmering in variations of black and silver.

'We're the sun and the moon,' Jas told him. 'Did you get it?'

Dad said he didn't get it immediately, but he did now.

'It's like we're magic.' Jas gazed at herself in the hall mirror. 'Nothing can hurt you when you're magic.'

I wish Jas could have seen the horse mural this morning, and the people's faces looking at it.

'They look real,' said the small volunteer. 'Are they going to stay here forever?'

'They'll wash away with the first rain,' I told her.

'But then what's the point?'

I don't know what the point is, why someone would go to all that trouble to make something that's only going to disappear. I only know that for the short time they will be there, despite the obvious hurry of the artist – the blurred edges, the hastily filled in background – those ponies gallop across that wall like they are about to burst out and charge straight at you, and while you are looking at them you forget about everything else, and that is magic too.

I sent Dodi a photograph of the drawings at the stable. I thought maybe that would show her how things hadn't changed – I mean, that I still hoped we were friends. That I want us to be friends.

'Still don't know who's doing it,' I wrote, but she hasn't answered.

Tom knows about the stables now, of course, because Dodi told him. But I've just remembered something – he can't have known about the drawings we did on the pavement, because he was in Bristol that weekend and by the time he came back to London, the rain had washed them all away.

Also I know that Tom doesn't like me like that, so I don't see why he would go about the place leaving drawings for me.

The zebra under our car.

The bluebells on the way to school.

The flowers and vines right outside our house.

The dachshund. Who else knows about the dachshund?

Think, think, think. When did the drawings first appear?

At the end of the summer holidays, the week before school started. When … oh my God! It can't be!

At the end of the summer holidays, the week before school started – when Marek moved into the square!

The Film Diaries of Bluebell Gadsby

Scene Seven
Horses Are Definitely Happier in the Country

Early morning, Horsehill Farm. Clear blue sky, pale gold sunlight, mist rising from the ground. The trees here have shed more leaves than those in London. Those that remain, in shades of red and yellow and orange, sway in a crisp autumn breeze.

Half a dozen ponies stand in the clean, swept yard between the stables and the paddock, tethered to the wooden fence. Inside the barn, the familiar figures of GLORIA, TWIG and the massive silhouette of Grandma's neighbour ISAMBARD HANRATTY are busying about. Twig spreads fresh straw in horseboxes. Gloria unpacks crates in the new tack room built last week by Isambard, who is nailing rows of hooks to the wall on which to hang halters and bridles.

CAMERAMAN (BLUEBELL)'s breath makes puffs of steam in the air. In the field beyond the paddock, SKYE HANRATTY (fourteen years old, no riding hat or saddle, sandy hair sticking straight up, wire-rimmed glasses held together with sticking plaster, a broad grin over newly acquired braces) and JASMINE are exercising horses. Manes fly, hooves thunder. Skye rides Tuesday, the black mare and biggest pony in the stables, but Jasmine on Mopsy is doing a fine job of keeping up as they tear around the field, her long hair streaming behind her like a banner from beneath her hat. The Dartmoor hills spread out beyond them in a circle of green and russet.

It is like the chalk drawing under the motorway come to life.

The ponies finish their lap of the field and decelerate like a car changing gears, from a gallop to a canter, a trot and then a jog and finally a walk as they file through the gate into the paddock where Cameraman is standing.

Skye and Jasmine are beaming. No – they are glowing, eyes bright, cheeks whipped to high colour by the exercise. As they lean down to pat their ponies' necks, to pull their ears and tug their manes and congratulate them, they don't look like riders at all. Rather, they are extensions of their mounts, so that it is almost a shock, when they slide off in the yard, to discover they have legs of their own and a human shape.

It is almost impossible to imagine two people looking more happy.

When we left Grandma at the end of the last holidays, she was all small and frail because she'd been ill and kept forgetting things. But when we arrived yesterday she was at the station with Zoran to meet us, looking a bit thin but otherwise exactly like she always has in her usual combination of pearls and gardening clothes, and not at all like a woman who needs looking after.

Last night at dinner, she sat at the head of the table tucking into Zoran's beef casserole like she hadn't eaten for weeks, firing away horse questions at Gloria like, WILL THE BLACK MARE FOAL NEXT SPRING? and SHOULD YOU TRY THE BROWN GELDING ON THE MARTINGALE? almost as loudly as she used to.

Horsehill has become completely horse mad.

Everyone is happy here. Pixie is happy because she says being here feels just like being with her family where she lives in the country in Ireland, and Pumpkin is happy because seeing so many ponies all together is blowing his tiny baby mind, and Twig is happy because when he is here he spends his whole time doing things like investigating natural science stuff like the lifecycle of newts or the nesting habits of barn owls, and not getting beaten up playing rugby. And Gloria is happy because she loves having so much space for the ponies, and Zoran is happy because he's always either playing the piano or cooking, when he isn't running down to the yard to kiss Gloria when he thinks nobody is looking.

Even Mum and Dad are happy, because they've stayed all alone in London for some Mum and Dad time, and happiest of all is Jas, who has morphed right back to being a half-wild person with tangled hair who spends her life galloping about on horseback wearing layers of torn multi-coloured jumpers over jodhpurs covered in mud and horse hair.

I am the only person, I think, who is not completely overjoyed to be here.

There's no Wi-Fi at Grandma's house (though Zoran says he's going to change that), and no mobile signal either. The only way you can actually send messages to anybody is using the broadband connection in Grandma's study, and even that's not easy because her life's mission has always been to shoo people outside because 'nothing beats fresh air and exercise'. I have been checking email and Facebook whenever I can get past Grandma, and this afternoon I took my phone on a walk up a hill to try to get some reception. I got three bars of signal for about half a minute, but Dodi still hasn't answered.

What if she never does?

Was it worth sacrificing our whole friendship just because she was a bit bossy?

Grandma came in as I was composing an email to Dodi, to send with a picture of the horses this morning, and asked what I was doing. When I explained, she said that it's difficult to be friends with someone who is very controlling, that if we were truly friends, then Dodi will forgive me and also that I should stop writing to her but talk to her face to face.

'But . . .'

Grandma took my hand off the mouse, turned off the computer and told me to go outside.

I've found Marek on Facebook. I want to write to him.

I want to ask, am I right? Is it you? And if it is, why do you do it?

The film I made this morning is pretty. What with the mist and the galloping horsemen, it looks mysterious and almost poetic. I wonder what Marek would think of it. I broke my rule of not sharing my films this afternoon and showed it to Skye when I came back from my walk.

'Do you like it?' I asked.

Skye looked out across the paddock to the field where half a dozen horses and ponies were grazing. Gloria and Zoran were walking towards them, hand in hand. The sun was already setting. The sky was darkening, touched with pink and gold around the edges, and our breath was coming out in puffs again.

'I do,' he said. 'But it's not as good as the real thing.'

I thought a lot of things when he said that.

I thought, I wonder what Marek would think of my film if I showed it to him?

I thought of his chalk ponies that looked like they were galloping to life underneath the motorway.

And I thought, I don't want to make films that are as good as the real thing.

I want to make films that are better.

Why do you draw in secret?

And why does he target me?

Tuesday 26 October

Jas drowned the hair straighteners today. We all had to witness it. She made us process from the paddock to the stream, with her leading the way on Mopsy and

Skye's dog Elsie trotting beside her and her tiara on her head instead of a riding hat, like a princess setting out to slay a dragon, except she wasn't carrying a sword but the hair straighteners on a ceremonial blue sofa cushion in front of her on the saddle.

She rode Mopsy right to the middle of the bridge over Grandma's stream, and then she held up a hand to tell us all to stop on the banks, and stood up in the stirrups with the cushion held out before her and shouted, 'I banish thee!'

Grandma asked, please could someone explain what was going on?

'We are here to banish Jas's demons,' Pixie explained. She had changed out of her usual boiler suit for the occasion, and was wearing a sort of black witch's cloak she had found in a charity shop in Plumpton, with a garland of ivy in her hair. Grandma said, please could someone else explain, because she failed to understand what demons had to do with hair curlers.

'They're not curlers, they're straighteners,' I told her. 'And they have been making Jas pretend she is something she's not.'

Gloria remarked you could hardly blame the straighteners. Twig agreed but said we couldn't very well drown Megan, Courtney, Chandra and Fran.

'Apart from it being illegal,' Twig said, 'they are not actually here.'

'Karma,' Pixie murmured, but no-one answered because this was the moment when Jas brandished the straighteners over her head and hurled them over the bridge and into the water.

'It's not very ecological,' Zoran said.

'She just wants to blow the electrics,' Twig said.

Then Jas recited a poem all about how bad straighteners are for hair, Twig fished them out of the stream, Isambard inspected them and said they were irreparable and they all went in for tea.

I didn't go with them. Instead I walked out on to the moor, up and up until I reached the top of the hill. It was freezing and a fog was coming in. I shouldn't have stayed – people lose their way and die on the moor every year in weather like that. But you feel so free, up there. I spread my arms and the wind rushed up and whipped my face, and my lungs filled with the damp, cold fog, and I ran in swooping circles pretending to be an aeroplane until I got dizzy, and crashed and lay on my back on the wet green grass alone in my whited-out world, laughing like a crazy person.

But then, when I'd finished laughing, I wanted to cry like I always do when I come here, because this was Iris's favourite place in the world, and it was so beautiful, and even if I could capture it on camera or turn it into a picture as perfect as Marek's, she would never see it.

Wednesday 27 October

I woke up before dawn to the sound of an engine outside my window, and when I opened my curtains there was Flora spilling out of a very old-looking car that was mainly blue but with one red door, dressed in her bunny rabbit onesie, snow boots, a duffle coat and a red tartan blanket. She saw me watching and waved. Other people started to climb out of the car after her.

'What?' I actually rubbed my eyes to make sure I wasn't hallucinating.

'Open the door!' she called up to me. 'We're dying of cold and I'm bursting for a pee!'

I tiptoed out of my room towards the stairs, but everyone was already awake.

'Is something wrong?' Zoran staggered on to the landing, rubbing his eyes.

'What on earth is that racket?' Grandma appeared in her dressing gown, clutching her walking stick like it was a weapon.

'FLORA'S HERE!' Jas's bedroom door burst open. In the dark behind, Twig groaned from under a heap of blankets. Outside, Flora and her friends were singing 'Frosty the Snowman' to keep warm. Pumpkin started to cry. In the bed next to his cot, Pixie started crooning. Gloria followed Zoran out on to the landing wearing her jodhpurs and mucking-out sweater.

'Might as well get up,' she yawned.

There were four drama students singing on the step when I opened the door – Flora, a massive bearded boy called Peter who looks like a bear, another boy called Barney with wild curly blond hair, and a beautiful girl with copper hair down to her waist and an old-fashioned velvet dress who said we should call her Maud, even though it's not her real name.

'Because of Maud Gonne,' Peter-the-bear explained. 'She was an Irish actress married to the poet W.B. Yeats. We all had to pick someone we admired at the beginning of term and think about how we would act them. She's been pretending to be Maud since September.'

'I love her,' Maud said simply.

'And I'm starving!' Flora cried. 'Is there any breakfast?'

They ate, and ate, and ate. They finished all

the eggs and all the bacon and all the bread. They used all the milk in big frothy cups of coffee and they devastated the fruit bowl and then, when they couldn't eat any more, Flora announced they had to sleep because they had been driving all night and were fit to drop.

'What are we going to eat?' Twig peered crossly at the empty fridge.

'We'll go to the shops after we've slept,' Flora promised.

'But I'm hungry now.'

Zoran asked how long was Flora planning on staying and where was she intending to sleep? Flora said she hadn't thought of that, she'd just come for a bit of a holiday and didn't we all think it was a lovely surprise?

'Are you on half-term?' Jas asked. 'We're staying until Sunday.'

She drooped a bit when she said that, I think because she remembered that Sunday is Halloween.

'We might be sort of just a tiny bit bunking off,' Flora admitted. She put her arms round Grandma. 'Don't tell Mum and Dad?'

Grandma, who adores Flora and intrigue and anything rebellious, said of course she wouldn't. Zoran gazed at her like he was saying please tell your grand-daughter this just isn't possible. Grandma, who was listening to Maud recite the poetry of W.B. Yeats, said nonsense, of course they could stay.

'Flora and Maud and Jas can move in with Blue,' Grandma said. 'And the boys can share with Twig. There's plenty of bedding.'

'But the cooking...'

'I'll help,' Barney said. 'I like cooking.'

And so they stayed, and took over the house. They slept all morning after breakfast, so Jas and Twig and I had to tiptoe in and out of our rooms to get dressed, and they never did make it to the shops. Instead when they woke up, they went to the pub, and they came back singing at five o'clock when it was getting dark, long after Zoran, Twig and I had been shopping and peeled a mountain of potatoes and chopped a tonne of onions and carrots and celery.

Barney didn't help to cook at all. Instead he sat in the bath for hours, using up all the hot water and playing his violin. Peter, who has the most delicate hands for a person so big, left a trail of wood shavings all over the kitchen, carving a horse for Jas out of a piece of wood he picked up on the way home from the pub, and Maud spooked the real horses by practising the trumpet out by the paddock.

And nobody minded. How could we? After dinner, while the rest of us washed up, Zoran played the piano while Barney played the fiddle. And after the washing up, Maud said we had to dance. 'Outside!' she insisted. 'By the light of the moon!'

We've danced outside at Horsehill, but never in winter, with the air so cold it burns your lungs and face and hands. And we've sung round the piano many times, but never so loud. It was two o'clock in the morning by the time we finally went to bed, Skye wobbling away to the Hanrattys' on his bicycle, Gloria grumbling that she had to be up again at dawn for the horses.

'I'll help you,' Maud promised. 'I'm good with horses.'

Gloria laughed. Maud tooted her trumpet, a single blast that made everybody jump.

I watched their faces, all of them, all through the evening. Peter, quiet and grave. Barney lost in music. Maud like some sort of ethereal, mischievous sprite. Flora quieter than usual. Skye for once not talking about horses. Gloria half asleep. Zoran thumping away at the piano. Grandma beaming. Twig laughing, his rugby bruises fading. Pixie with Pumpkin on her lap, clapping to the music. Jas with her curls bouncing back.

I wanted to film them, but I didn't dare, not in front of Flora's friends. But there was something in the air tonight, something I wish I'd caught. Something unreal and bigger than us all.

Thursday 28 October

It was raining this morning. Skye (who is paid) worked in the yard, and Maud kept her promise to help Gloria, but Barney and Twig stayed in bed while Flora, Peter, Jas and I drove round sodden country lanes and tramped the dripping streets of Plumpton, distributing leaflets for Gloria announcing that the Horsehill School of Riding would shortly be open for business. Afterwards we huddled .....into a café with steamed-up windows and lots of shivering, damp-looking tourists and soggy paper ghosts decorating the walls, where Flora ordered tea for everybody and asked what the plan was for Halloween.

Jas started stabbing the sugar bowl with her spoon. 'What's everyone going dressed as?' Flora continued. 'Have you got your costumes yet?'

Jas finished murdering the sugar and started shredding paper napkins as the whole Cupcake Crew story came out.

'Why didn't you tell me all this?' Flora demanded again when Jas had finished.

Jas hung her head.

'Why didn't you tell me?' she demanded, glaring at me.

'I tried to!' I protested. 'You were doing that stupid silent week.'

'You put leaflets in everybody's lockers? You wrote a poem?'

Jas mumbled that it was a good poem, and that it had taken her ages to write it. Peter laughed. Flora buried her face in her hands.

'You told me to stand up for myself!' Jas protested.

'Not like that!' Flora cried. 'Anonymous leaflets... Jas, it's so sneaky.'

'The wings weren't sneaky,' I said. 'The wings were brave.'

'Yes.' Jas had gone all droopy, and Flora's expression softened as she looked at her. 'The wings were brave. OK, let's think about this. There has to be something we can do.'

She pressed her head in her hands again. We all watched and waited.

'I've got it!' Flora slapped the table, and we all jumped. 'Jazzcakes, the wings were brave. The problem is they were also too small. They weren't enough of a statement. Let's go!'

We splashed after her down Plumpton High Street.

'Where are we going?' I panted.

'In here!' Flora stopped so suddenly we all crashed into her.

'The charity shop?'

'It's where Pixie bought that cloak.'

She pushed open the door and waved us all in. We stood dripping in the middle of the shop. The sales assistant looked dismayed.

'Jazzcakes,' Flora announced, 'we are going to get you the best flipping Halloween outfit those girls have ever seen.'

We put on a talent show this evening. We pushed back all the furniture in the lounge and Peter rigged up poles and sheets and bedspreads as a stage, and almost everyone took turns to perform.

Zoran played the piano. He opened with 'Frosty the Snowman', which made everyone laugh, then played some of his old ragtime favourites like 'The Entertainer', then he accompanied Jas as she recited one of her poems, and Pixie doing a series of acrobatic yoga exercises. Twig did a card trick, and Skye told a joke about a greyhound, a camel and a horse (even though I told him a million times it wasn't funny).

Barney played his fiddle and Maud played her trumpet, and Gloria sang a song in Spanish she said was all about gypsies and mountains and people murdering each other, and Isambard and Lizzie sang a duet from their favourite opera, and Grandma told a scary old Dartmoor story about a witch.

If Marek were here, I thought, out of nowhere, he would read *Of Mice and Men*.

Then Flora made everybody laugh with funny dances imitating different animals like penguins and elephants and even a sloth.

'I didn't know Flora could dance,' I said to Peter.

'She's great, isn't she?' he said.

Peter and I were the only ones who didn't have an act. He worked away quietly in the background all evening, changing lighting and moving furniture around so that everyone could do their turn properly, while I filmed everything. Then afterwards, while we were clearing up, he asked if I ever wanted to be in front of the camera rather than behind it.

'It's not my thing,' I said, and then I started to blush, because he asked what was my thing, and I wanted to ask him if he agreed with Zoran, about film being like art and all that, but I didn't know how without sounding totally up myself.

'Can I see?' Peter held his hand out to my camera, and I shook my head.

'I don't like showing my work,' I said, and then we both burst out laughing, because that did sound up myself, and also because I realised as I said it how it didn't make sense, because what's the point of making films that no-one is going to watch?

It's even more pointless than drawings that get washed away by the rain.

'What sort of films do you want to make?' Peter asked.

I have often noticed how laughing makes you not afraid any more.

'Films that are better than real life,' I said. I thought about what Zoran said about art, ages ago, when he was trying to help Jas with her art project. 'Films that change people's lives.'

Peter stacked the last sheet on top of its pile. He picked up the whole stack, but instead of leaving to take them upstairs he just stood there, staring out of the window at the night, and said, 'One day, we'll all make a film together. I'll design it and that lot' – he pointed at Flora and Maud and Barney – 'will star, and your camera will turn the whole thing into a work of beauty.'

'Work of beauty!' I tried not to look too pleased.

Peter, who is a very practical person, said that if I

really wanted to make films, I should apply to do a summer course next year at the South Bank School of Film Studies.

'I'm not good enough!' I protested.

'You'll never know if you don't try.' He nudged me, just like Zoran does. 'You'll see, Blue,' he promised. 'One day you'll make history.'

He's mad of course. There is no way I am good enough, but still . . . My mind is going crazy, shooting off into daydreams. Mum and Dad crying at my Oscars acceptance speech . . . A premiere at an Imax cinema, a red carpet and me in a glittering dress and journalists all whispering, 'Who is she?'

'Don't you know?' one of them will say. 'THAT is the famous camerawoman, Blue Gadsby.' My life, like a fabulous Hollywood movie.

You'll make history. The way Peter said it, I almost believe him.

Friday 29 October

A parade. That is Flora's plan.

Halloween is on Sunday evening. We go home on Sunday morning. Between now and then, it's all about the costumes.

'What about Zoran and Gloria and the stables?' I asked.

'Be reasonable, Blue. Do they need us?'

'But I don't want to be in a parade,' Twig protested. 'I'm supposed to be doing Halloween with the rugby team. It's important. It's like a bonding exercise.'

Flora said the rugby team could join us as long as they do exactly what she says, and that we all had to pull together. Even the drama students are involved.

'Can Todd come too?' Jas asked, and Flora cried sure, the more the merrier.

I'm a little bit worried about this whole operation.

Peter has taken over the costumes. We found lots of stuff in the charity shop, and also in Grandma's attic. We have a tutu and a top hat, Pixie's cloak and a short scarlet cape, a man's tweed suit and a Victorian lady's riding habit, a bridal veil and a gas mask, a gold-fringed shawl and a length of purple velvet.

I don't see how this all fits together, but Flora says we are going to put on the best Halloween display Chatsworth Square has ever seen, and show those cupcake madams once and for all just how little Jas needs them.

'That way they will leave you alone for good,' Flora said.

'Are you sure about this?' I asked her this evening, as Peter measured Pumpkin up for his costume (as well as being good at sets, he is excellent with a sewing machine).

Flora asked, 'Sure about what?' I said it just seemed like a lot. Flora said, 'A lot of what?'

I thought of Dodi, who has still not answered any of my messages.

'A lot that could go wrong,' I said.

Flora said nonsense, and we had to stand united before the cupcake girls to show them Jas could not be crushed.

'I'm just not convinced it's always a good idea to stand up to people,' I said. 'I think sometimes it can backfire.'

'The trouble with you, Blue,' Flora said, 'is you lack ambition.'

'I'm extremely ambitious!' I protested, but as usual she didn't listen.

Sunday 31 October

It's early in the morning, and I am writing from the train.

Flora made us leave two hours before we had planned this morning, to make sure we have plenty of time to get ready for the parade. She left even earlier than us in the car with the drama students. They are going to get ready at her friend Tamsin's house, and meet us at five o'clock in our costumes in the mews by the church in Chatsworth Square.

'Why don't you get ready at home?' Jas asked, but Flora said it was probably best if she came home later rather than sooner.

'Because she's supposed to be in Scotland,' Twig said.

'Just pretend it's a normal Halloween,' Flora said. 'Carve pumpkins. Buy trick or treat stuff. Then get dressed and come and find us.'

Everyone is nervous.

I am nervous in case Dodi will be in Chatsworth Square and won't want to talk to me, and also in case Marek sees us and thinks we are ridiculous.

Twig is nervous because Flora has persuaded him to ask the rugby team to join in the parade, and they are all coming to our house this afternoon to get ready, and he has to convince them to let him put makeup on them.

And Jas is the most nervous of all, because of the sheer scale of what Flora wants us to do.

The Film Diaries of Bluebell Gadsby

Scene Eight
A Halloween to Remember

Early evening. The sky is dark
above London. Thanks to Mrs Doriot-
Buffet's leaflets, the normally
sedate Chatsworth Square has been
transformed into a sort of parallel
universe as scores of residents have
risen to the challenge of decorating
their houses.

Only the church on the north side of
the square is in darkness (the local
vicar not approving of the living
dead).

Exceptionally, the square has been
closed to traffic. Fake spider webbing
swathes rosebushes. A rubber corpse
swings from a lamp post. Oversized

papier-mâché bats hang from trees. Houses are garlanded with glow-in-the-dark skulls. Flickering pumpkins adorn doorsteps. Children dressed as skeletons and witches, vampires and ghosts, fairies and princesses and monsters, dart in groups from door to door like shoals of exotic fish gathering sweets, followed by sheepish-looking grown-ups in pointy hats. Teenagers too old for trick or treating roam the streets in packs.

A girl with devil's horns and a black netting skirt reapplies grey lipstick using her mobile phone as a mirror. A nurse covered in fake blood shares a can of drink with a boy in a leopard print waistcoat with whiskers painted on his face, and a hammer in his head. Four zombie schoolgirls with back-combed hair and knee-high white socks swish by, stuffing their faces with loot from their trick or treat bags.

They are MEGAN, COURTNEY, CHANDRA and FRAN.

In the heart of the square, behind their iron railings, the communal gardens are in darkness. If you stop to listen, you can hear rustling in the bushes. High above, plane trees sway. Camera lingers before returning to the thronging streets.

Six o'clock. It's time. CAMERAMAN (BLUEBELL, dressed in a man's three-piece suit and beret in the manner of iconic American comic Buster Keaton in his film *The Cameraman*, with white stage makeup, hollowed-out dark-rimmed eyes, talcum-powdered hair and gold lipstick) runs up the steps of the church and turns towards the entrance of the tiny church mews.

A trumpet blast tears through the air. All around the square, monsters and werewolves and ghouls stop wandering.

All eyes turn towards the church.

Another trumpet blast, and FLORA's parade emerges from the mews, marching to the sound of Barney's violin.

It is – they are – magnificent.

They process in the flickering light of live flame torches held aloft by Flora in a tutu and gas mask, and PETER in a scarlet cape and top hat, while BARNEY (in a tweed suit) plays on his fiddle and MAUD in her riding habit sounds her trumpet, and PIXIE in her witch's cloak carries a wide-awake PUMPKIN in a purple velvet sleeping bag with demon's wings on his back. Behind them, fifteen boys in full rugby kit toss a ball back and forth, painted silver to reflect the firelight.

At the head of the procession marches JASMINE. She wears a white satin dress carefully shredded by Peter, so that long tendrils flutter as she walks, over black leggings decorated with silver spiders and her favourite silver high-tops. On her head, thrown back from her face and secured by her tiara, she wears Grandma's wedding veil. Beside her, in an army uniform much too big for him, TODD waves Grandpa's ancient regimental banner.

They all wear the same dramatic makeup as Cameraman.

They are an army of ghosts, unified by death.

The crowds part to let them pass. A gaggle of ghouls start to cheer. They pass the four zombie schoolgirls. Jasmine (not very subtly) grins. Maud toots her trumpet in their faces. They scream. People laugh. The parade passes DODI, JAKE, COLIN and TOM, all wearing bowler hats and fake glasses and moustaches.

Dodi's moustachioed face is expressionless as she stares back at the camera, but the boys cheer and join in the procession. Tom catches the rugby ball and tosses it to TWIG, who is leading the team. Twig fumbles and drops it. Another player picks it up and lobs it back. One of his teammates jumps to catch it like he's in the line-up on the field.

A vaguely familiar large woman in a Venetian mask and gold cape asks Flora if she has a permit for those torches.

Flora ignores her. Maud blows a comedy tune on her trumpet. Handsome MAX, who lives at number 72 and is dressed as Prince Charming with a rope around his neck, runs out of a house carrying a fiddle and starts to play alongside Barney.

The large woman in Venetian mask and gold cape strides towards them. Her size and American accent reveal her to be Mrs Doriot-Buffet.

MRS DORIOT-BUFFET
Those torches are a fire hazard!

The fiddling grows faster and louder. The rugby boys start a conga line. A few of them trip and fall out. The ball throwing grows wilder.

They are passing the entrance to the communal gardens when the ball sails overhead and disappears into the darkness. One of the rugby boys swears. His friends give him a leg-up over the wall. The parade moves on, but Cameraman remains standing.

She zooms in on the door which stands in the brick wall of the communal gardens.

A door which on any other day is just a door, plain and wooden and unadorned, but which tonight . . .

Tonight the door is woven with ivy and lilies. A squirrel clings to it upside down, bushy tail curling round railings that should not be there. A robin cocks its head, bright eyes inviting. Something very like a pixie peers out from behind the foliage.

The door is no longer a door.

It is a gateway to another world.

Cameraman steps closer.

It is made entirely of chalk.

Cameraman scans the crowd now. She is looking for Dodi or Marek, but as the silver ball flies back over the wall, she is forced to return her attention to the parade. The ball clips Flora on the shoulder. She swings round, still brandishing her torch.

FLORA

For goodness sake, Twig, can't you
control them?

TWIG

I'm not captain! You're the one who
said they could come!

The rugby team break into song.

And now Pumpkin has had enough and begins to cry. Pixie announces she has to take him home. Prince Charming and Barney have stopped playing their fiddles and look like they might be about to kiss. The rugby players have started a scrum. Todd lowers his banner. Jas looks at Flora as if to say, 'Now what?'

From behind Flora, sparks begin to fly. Smoke wafts upwards. Something crackles as flames grow taller, feeding on privet hedge and fake spider webbing and papier-mâché bats.

MRS DORIOT-BUFFET

My house! My garden! My decorations!

She sprints into her house and emerges with a garden hose. She sprays water over the fire. It goes out, but the decorations are ruined.

                    MRS DORIOT-BUFFET
                (turns her hose on Flora)
            I told you those flames were
            dangerous! I should report you to
                        the police!

                        DODI
                (emerging from the crowd)
            Oh for heaven's sake! It's not that
                        bad!

                    MRS DORIOT-BUFFET
            You two! I might have known! Never
            come near my home again!

She turns her jet on the disintegrating parade. The rugby team are rolling on the ground, getting as dirty as possible. Pixie hurries away with Pumpkin. Flora has started to scream unrepeatable names at Mrs Doriot-Buffet, who is screaming back, still spraying. Jake, Colin and Tom are cheering and eating miniature chocolate bars from a pumpkin-shaped bag they found abandoned in the street.

Jas stands apart from the others, away from the water jet, but it is already too late. Makeup runs down her face. Her wet veil is plastered to her hair. All her earlier poise has gone – no longer a bride from beyond the grave, but a little girl in ripped-up second-hand clothes. She is not crying, but her lower lip wobbles dangerously.

The zombie schoolgirls smirk, triumphant.

The crowd parts again, and the Gadsby children's MOTHER appears.

Mum loved our costumes when we showed her them before going out, and she didn't mind at all about the rugby boys (who were very well behaved), but she was furious about the fire, and mystified about Flora's presence.

'Torches!' she cried. 'Fiddles and trumpets and setting fire to things!'

Dad, who thought the whole thing was splendid (his word), tried to placate her by saying how creative the whole parade idea was.

'Creative! A house nearly burned down!'

Flora said that was a bit of an exaggeration. Mum turned on her.

'What are you even *doing* here, Flora? You say you're on holiday, but I don't remember seeing any mention of half-term when we looked at term dates.'

Barney, Peter and Maud started shuffling towards the door.

'We'd better go,' Maud said.

'Class tomorrow,' Barney agreed.

'Long drive,' Peter murmured.

Flora tried to back out of the room with them.

'And that's it?' Mum cried, unreasonably. 'You're leaving, just like that?'

Flora turned back. In the hall outside, the others froze. For a very short moment, no-one spoke.

Then Flora said, 'Actually, I'm not going back to Scotland,' and Mum went nuts again.

Twig and I tiptoed out with Maud, Peter and Barney and walked them round the corner to the blue car with the red door.

'What's going on with Flora?' I asked Peter, but he said that she should be the one to tell us.

'So long, camera girl.' He pulled me into an enormous hug. 'I'm looking forward to that film we're going to make together one day.'

'Me too,' I said, and then they were gone.

As we turned for home, a group of zombie rugby players ran past us, still tossing the silver ball back and forth across the street.

'Do you want to join them?' I asked Twig, but he shook his head.

'I dropped the ball,' he whispered. 'When Tom threw it to me. Did you see?'

I wasn't sure what to say, because obviously I did see – I even caught it on film.

'Anyone would have dropped it,' I said, but Twig just sighed and looked depressed.

When we got back Jas and Pixie were sitting on the landing in their dressing gowns, with most but not all their makeup scrubbed off, listening to Mum and Dad and Flora shout at each other in the living room.

'Flora has come back to do Angel's play,' Jas whispered to us. 'She's been doing rehearsals by Skype.'

'Is that even possible?'

'That's what Dad asked, but Flora says yes. The play opens in two weeks, and after it's finished Flora says she's going to stay.'

Downstairs, the noise was getting worse.

'We have paid for a whole year of tuition!' Mum cried. 'You begged and begged and said this was what you wanted!'

'I'm sorry!' Flora didn't sound sorry at all. 'I'll pay you back!'

'WITH WHAT MONEY?'

'The money I make from the play!'

Mum started to laugh like a crazy person.

'Cassie.' Dad's voice was unusually firm. 'Let her do this. Then we can talk about what she wants to do next.'

'This is what I want,' Flora said. 'The real thing. Not tongue massages and breathing exercises. Proper acting.'

Jas shivered and sneezed. Pixie stood up and

pulled her to her feet. 'A hot bath,' Pixie said. 'I have some herbs you can put in it to stop you getting a cold.'

Twig and I followed. There seemed no point in staying. No-one can ever get in Flora's way when she's made her mind up about something.

Later, when things had calmed down and we'd had dinner and done some of the homework we should have done in the holidays, and Flora was happy again because Mum and Dad agreed to let her do the play, I went in to see Jas.

Her eyes were red and her nose was running, and she kept either blowing it or sniffing.

'I've got a cold,' she said. 'Pixie's herbs didn't work.'

I pretended to believe her.

'The parade was great,' I said, but I was lying too, and she knew it.

Afterwards, when Jas had gone to bed, I went through my film of Halloween. There were Flora and Jas and all the others, splendid in their costumes, and there was Mrs Doriot-Buffet and the rugby team and Prince Charming and his violin, and the door to the gardens with the ivy and pixies and robin, but however hard I looked, I couldn't find a single sign of Marek Valenta. I zoomed in on the fire, but instead of looking at the burning hedge, focused on his house next door.

There were no decorations outside, and only one light, right on the top floor.

Was it his?

Oh God . . . if the fire had been worse, Flora could have set fire to his house!

My phone pinged. A message from Dodi, with a photograph. Her and me and Iris, eight years old, dressed up as ghosts for Halloween with sheets over our heads with cauldron-shaped trick or treat bags.

The message just said, 'Meet me before school?'

It didn't say where, but I already knew.

There is only one place.

'Eight o'clock,' I replied.

Dodi wrote, 'I'll bring snacks.'

Monday 1 November

The place is the bit in the park where nobody is allowed to go, where the gardeners keep their tools and machinery.

It is the place we always used to come with Iris, when there were important things to say.

The place where she was going on the night she

was hit by a van, on her way to rescue some baby foxes born at the wrong time of year.

We haven't been back there since she died four years ago. I wasn't even sure you could still get in. The hole in the fence we used to squeeze through when we were children has been blocked off, but we're bigger now, and when I got there this morning I realised how easy it was to climb over.

Dodi was already there, wiping dirt off her jeans. As I jumped down beside her, she held up a packet of Bourbon biscuits and two cartons of Ribena.

'Oh!' Something caught in my throat. 'You remembered.'

'They were her favourites,' Dodi said. 'Of course I remember.'

We sat with our backs against the gardeners' shed and our faces tilted towards the morning sun, nibbling the biscuits the way Iris used to until only the filling was left.

'I'm sorry for being mean,' I said at last. 'For making you split up with Jake.'

'No, I'm sorry,' Dodi said. 'For going on about Tom when you kept telling me you didn't like him.'

I didn't want to say any more after that, but in my mind I could hear Grandma saying, 'It's difficult being friends with someone who is always controlling you,' and I knew that if I wanted us to carry on being friends, I had to.

'It's just,' I started. 'I mean … I don't think you realise, but you're a bit …'

'What?'

'Bossy. It makes me feel a bit …'

'What?'

'Bullied.'

'Bullied?'

Dodi looked so upset I wanted to take it all back, but I bit my lip.

'I would never bully you! Blue, you're my best friend!'

'I know! I know, I'm just saying … Because you're my best friend too.'

Dodi stared at her carton of juice. Then she put it down on the ground in front of her, next to the half empty packet of biscuits, so she could lay her hands over them both, and turned to look at me.

'On Iris's memory,' she vowed, 'I swear that I will never crush you or boss you or bully you again.'

I put my hands over hers. 'And I swear I will never let you, but that if you are, I will not be mean or cause you to split up with your boyfriend.'

Iris would have laughed at us, swearing over her favourite snacks. We almost laughed too, except for the tears in our eyes. Then Dodi sniffed, and we finished the biscuits, and slurped the juice, and realised we were going to be late for school.

'I'm actually back with Jake,' she said, as we hurried down the Avenue.

'I wondered,' I said. 'I saw you at Halloween. I didn't know if you were just friends.'

'He wouldn't talk to me all half-term. But then yesterday he came round and said he still wanted to go out with me, but that he promised to not be so serious if that was what I wanted. And I realised . . .'

She stopped.

'What?'

'I realised I don't mind him being serious. I think I was just . . . I was just afraid before, because I think – I think I'm in love with him, Blue. I've never been in love with anyone before.'

'Wow,' I said. 'Dodi. I'm so happy for you!'

But I think that was enough emotion for Dodi for one morning, because she just gave herself a little 'pull yourself together' shake and said, 'Explain last night, because that was completely mental.'

I explained how it was Flora's idea, to show the Cupcake Girls what Jas was capable of.

'It may have worked.' I tried to keep the doubt out of my voice. 'I guess we'll find out after school.'

Dodi snorted and said of course it hadn't worked. 'And I'll tell you why,' she said. I think that however hard she tries Dodi will always sound bossy. 'It's because it wasn't about what Jas can do at all. It was about Flora. It was typical Flora. "Look at me, how amazing I am." What Jas should have done is be normal. Dressed up like a witch or a vampire like every other ten-year-old, and hung out with her friends and stuffed her face with sweets. Now she has to lie low. And when I say low, I mean practically underground. When you're up against cupcake girls, you can't win. All you can do is stay out of their way.'

Which is easy for her to say. No-one I know would ever dare to mess with Dodi Cartwright.

'She can't just give up,' I said. 'She can't just let them win. Look at . . .'

Look at us, I was going to say. What would have happened to us if I hadn't stood up to you? You would have carried on bossing me around, and I would have got more and more resentful, or possibly even ended up going out with Tom . . . But we had stopped at the crossroads, waiting for the lights to change, and Dodi was staring at her phone with a soft expression on her face, reading a text from Jake.

I didn't say anything. Instead, as we hurried into

school, I asked 'Did you see the fairy portal last night?'

'Fairy portal?'

I started to explain about the chalk drawing, but Jake was walking towards us across the playground, and Dodi – as usual – wasn't listening.

Marek doodles all the time. How could I never have noticed? I watched him in the classes we had together. He never stops. I always thought he must be as swotty as Hattie, whose note-taking skills are so legendary they were actually once the subject of an entire assembly, but if you bother to look properly when you think he is writing he is actually drawing. I tried to peep over his shoulder in Maths when I went to sharpen my pencil, but he slammed his book shut.

I just thought – he hadn't even met me when I saw the first drawing – the zebra under the car. He didn't even know me!

Does that mean it isn't him? But the doodling... the dachshund... the ponies!

He sits in class, impeccably dressed in those clothes no-one else our age would ever wear, his hair perfectly combed and his shoes perfectly polished, and I can't imagine him stealing out at night, chalks in hand, to draw dogs or bluebells or galloping ponies. But then I think of Marek watching us in the park. Of Marek at our party – *Do you miss Prague? Very much.*

There are hidden depths to Marek Valenta. The question is, how do you discover them?

Wednesday 3 November

Flora had her first non-Skype rehearsal yesterday. She was still giddy with it this morning.

'I love Peter and Barney and Maud,' she burbled over breakfast. 'They're lovely. Everyone on my course is lovely. But they're babies, you know? The people in Angel's play are grown-ups. Real actors. Just one rehearsal and I can feel myself . . .' She took a deep breath.

'Growing,' Pixie said.

'Exactly!' Flora beamed at her.

'How long is she staying?' Twig muttered, as we left for school. 'Because I thought I was glad to see her, but now she's driving me nuts.'

Dad called Ms Foulkes-Watson on Monday morning, and she was categorical. 'Flora can choose,' she said. 'Drama school, which will provide her with tools for a long acting career, or a one-off part in a two-bit production only a handful of people will see.'

'It is Shakespeare,' Dad pointed out, but Ms Foulkes-Watson said any fool can put on *Romeo and Juliet*, and Angel del Castro was famous for what she called, 'disastrous experimental productions'.

'Trust me,' she said. 'Nobody will see it.'

Mum says she doesn't know if she is more furious or disappointed. Dad says there's no point forcing Flora to do anything she doesn't want to do. Flora is walking on air.

I think Jas is happier now. On Monday morning, I thought she was going to be sick. Literally. She came down dressed entirely in black, with her hair in plaits tied with red ribbons and her face slightly green. After school, when we tried to ask her about her day, she just said 'fine' and stuck her chin out and refused to give any details but later on I'm sure I heard her crying in her bedroom, and I didn't know how to make her feel better. But then today when she came home, she sat down at the kitchen table, pulled her writing book out of her school bag and started scribbling away.

'What are you writing?' I asked.

'Please tell me it's not another poem about the cupcake girls,' Twig whispered.

'I can hear you, Twig,' Jas said. 'And I'm not stupid. This has nothing to do with them. It's for a poet called Nancy Chikado who is coming to visit school on Friday.'

'I think that's a brilliant idea, Jas.' I tried to smile encouragingly at Jas at the same time as I frowned at Twig. 'She'll love that.'

'She is amazing,' Jas said. 'She grew up in a refugee camp, and came here when she was fourteen years old all on her own without her family, and she wrote poetry the whole time. She says that writing poetry saved her, because when she was writing she stopped thinking about how awful everything was, and tried to focus on what was beautiful. Poetry saved her, Blue.'

'Poetry hasn't saved you,' Twig pointed out. 'It's only got you into trouble.'

Jas told him he didn't understand a thing.

The Film Diaries of Bluebell Gadsby

Scene Nine
Of Mice and Men

Evening, a London West End theatre. It is the interval in the middle of the dramatisation of Steinbeck's *Of Mice and Men*, and the oak-panelled, heavily mirrored, red-carpeted foyer is swarming with fourteen and fifteen-year-olds, all brought here by enthusiastic English teachers and all, truthfully, more excited by the prospect of sweets and ice-cream than by the play itself. The noise levels, as they swarm around ushers with their trays of goodies, are deafening.

Alone and unnoticed, CAMERAMAN (BLUEBELL) ignores her fellow students and instead focuses her camera on the wooden skirting, where a paper cut-out of a chalk mouse is stuck to the wall. She follows the direction in which it is pointing. Beyond the sweeping staircase, by the theatre doors, there is an identical drawing. She walks over to it and out into the street. The next mouse is not on paper, but drawn directly on to the pavement, at the corner of a dark and shady alley.

Cameraman hesitates. Should she go in? On the one hand, she has to know what this is leading to. On the other – it's a dark and shady alley . . .

Curiosity wins. Cameraman steps into the alley, which after a few feet opens into a scruffy yard at the back of the theatre. There are wheelie bins and a fire escape, and almost certainly rats. Cigarette ends litter the ground, empty coffee takeout cups, a crushed drinks can. Double doors into the theatre, wide enough for the most extravagant sets, are closed. It is a world away from the bright lights, the bars and cafés, clubs and theatres of Shaftesbury Avenue.

Cameraman scans the walls. Two more mice, pointing the way towards another passageway at the back of the yard. Her heart thumps. What if, in the dark, a murderer lurks, waiting to pounce?

But why would a murderer lure her here with pictures of mice?

Telling herself to be brave, Cameraman creeps closer and peers into the passageway.

And gasps. Because there before her, finally, is her proof.

Marek Valenta stands with his back to her, drawing. At his feet lie his perfectly tailored coat and his grown-up cashmere scarf. On the wall before him, in white chalk on dirty London brick, a chalk giant of a man is materialising. He wears rumpled dungarees, heavy work boots, a soft brown hat. Sitting on his outstretched hand, so lifelike you can almost see his whiskers quiver, is the final mouse.

Cameraman catches her breath. Marek Valenta's hand freezes. Then slowly, slowly, he turns around.

We stared at each other for ages.

I reached out to touch the mouse. Brushed chalk off my hands. Turned to stare at him again. He was very pale – even paler than usual – his teeth biting his lower lip as he watched me.

'Do you like it?' he asked.

'I love it,' I said.

A voice crashed into the quiet of the yard – Miss Foundry, looking for us.

'Quick,' I said. 'Before she sees the picture.'

We squeezed into our seats with seconds to spare.

'Where were you?' Dodi asked.

'I just went for a walk.'

On stage, people shot each other and shouted and died, but I barely even noticed. A few seats down from me, Marek sat with his eyes fixed on the actors, and my head whirled with questions.

The same questions as always.

Why do you do it?

Why me?

I'll talk to him on the Tube on the way home, I thought, but when we came out there was a massive black four-by-four waiting in front of the theatre, blocking the traffic, with Mr Valenta in a navy blue coat and his Paris trilby jumping up and down in front of it, waving.

For a moment, I thought Marek was going to turn back into the theatre, but Mr Valenta spotted him and started shouting 'Marek! Marek! Over here!' and he was forced to go outside.

'We have been to the opera!' Mr Valenta cried. He looked different from when he came to our house. Sort of ... happy. I remembered what Mrs Valenta had said about him wanting to study music. Maybe the opera had put him in a good mood. 'We came to collect you so you could ride with us!'

Tom clapped a sympathetic hand on Marek's shoulder, pushing him towards the car. Mr Valenta looked at him suspiciously. Tom saluted and clicked his heels. Jake and Colin burst out laughing and also saluted.

'Don't!' I protested.

'It's only a joke! He looks so ...'

'What?'

'So rich.'

'Well it's not funny.'

They didn't see Marek's face as he got into the car, bright with embarrassment and anger and nothing like the boy I saw during the interval, drawing a giant and a mouse on the wall of a darkened alley.

'Strange boy.' Dodi was standing beside me, watching me. I turned away so she wouldn't see me blush.

I thought Jas really was ill this morning, because she came down for breakfast looking very, very pale, and didn't eat a thing even though Flora got up specially to make her pancakes. She just sat in her chair looking very small, staring straight ahead with enormous dark eyes and looking like a hummingbird or maybe a tiny parrot, because she was dressed from head to toe in her brightest clothes, including her pink and orange tights and her rainbow hair ribbon.

'What is going on?' I asked, as Flora cut up pancakes and made clucking sounds to try to make Jas eat.

Twig said that today was the day that the refugee poet Nancy Chikado was going to Jas's school, and that Miss Jamison (the librarian who loves poetry) liked the poem Jas wrote for her so much she asked Jas to read it in assembly in front of the whole school.

'And the . . .' I gestured discreetly towards Jas's outfit.

'Nancy Chikado loves colours. She's famous for it. She says they remind her of her home.'

We watched in silence as Jas took a minuscule sip of water from her glass, then ran towards the bathroom.

'Stage fright,' Flora said, scoffing Jas's untouched pancakes. 'She'll be fine once she gets started.'

I didn't think about Jas again until this afternoon, because the minute I got to school all I could think about was seeing Marek. Then, when I did see him, I didn't know where to look and spent the whole day trying to avoid him, but also sort of hoping he would talk to me, and laughing too loudly whenever he was near so he wouldn't realise all I could actually think of was him, and the drawing of Lennie and the mouse.

Do you like it? I love it.

What else could I have said? Should I have said?

It's so good. You are obviously very talented at drawing. I am extremely impressed.

Why did you draw a zebra with a bluebell in its mouth?

I too would like to be an artist.

It was exhausting.

It never occurred to me that Jas wouldn't be fine, because she's recited poetry in front of people before, but when I got home I saw at once that things were extremely wrong.

Flora went to see her with Mum and Dad, and she told Twig and me everything.

The assembly hall was packed, Flora said. It's not big enough to hold the whole school but every single child was there to see the poet, from the tinies right through to Year Six, sitting on benches at the back and on the floor at the front and crammed into every inch of space, all facing the stage.

'It smelled of feet,' Flora said. 'I'd forgotten that about school. Feet, and a sort of cabbage.'

'But what happened?' Twig asked, because Jas was lying face down on the sofa but nobody had told us why yet.

'Jas did really well,' Flora said. 'Honestly, you would never believe how nervous she was this morning. She wasn't shaking at all. I could tell, you know, because she was holding her poem, and the paper was completely still. She went right to the middle of the stage, like she's supposed to, and then ...'

And then, just as she was about to begin, there was a commotion at the back of the hall and Megan, Courtney, Chandra and Fran appeared. All dressed completely unlike themselves in the loudest colours you could imagine, and calling, 'Sorry sorry sorry' as they squished and squashed just about the entire school, ignoring the teachers trying to catch them, until they arrived right at the front, brandishing a huge white cardboard box.

Ms Smokey, who is the Headteacher, asked what on earth were the girls doing and please could they sit down. Megan said they just had a present for Miss Chikado and they spent ages doing it and please could they give it to her? Ms Smokey started to say, 'Later, please go and sit down' but Megan was already on the stage, and Courtney was handing her the box, and Nancy Chikado was opening it and exclaiming oh, how lovely! and showing it to everyone, and it was full of . . .

'Cupcakes!' Flora said. 'Dozens of them, in every hideous colour you can imagine.'

Jas whimpered, still on the sofa. Flora stroked her head like she was a cat.

The hall went wild when the cupcakes appeared. The younger kids were all, 'Can I have one?' and the older ones were all, 'Yay, we can make noise because the younger kids are,' and by the time Miss Jamison said, 'Now Jas is going to read us her poem,' the bell was ringing for morning lessons and Jas was looking ill again.

'She couldn't say a single word,' Flora whispered. 'She just stood there on stage with her mouth opening and closing like a goldfish and not a squeak coming out, and those monster cupcake girls just watching, swishing their hair about with horrible smug smiles on their horrible faces.'

Jas's wardrobe is practically empty now. I went into her room this evening to check she was all right, and found her once again surrounded by a pile of clothes to throw out. Except this time they weren't the drab, sensible things she doesn't like to wear, and they certainly weren't the new pastel hoodies she made Mum buy her so she could look like the cupcake girls. They were her stripy tights and her green jumper, her purple leggings and her too-small dress, Flora's old lacy cardigan and the rainbow ribbon.

'But they're your happy clothes,' I said.

Jas said she didn't care, and she was never going to wear them again.

Saturday 6 November

There are fireworks in the park tonight for Bonfire Night. Flora tried to convince Jas to go with her.

'There's a fair!' Flora said. 'Music, candy-floss, people, fun!'

'Everyone from school will be there,' Jas said.

'You can't avoid your whole school for ever.'

'I'm not going.'

'Come with me,' Twig said. 'I'm going with the rugby boys. We'll protect you.'

Dropping the rugby ball during the Halloween parade doesn't seem to have damaged Twig's standing with the team at all. Apparently, they keep telling him how awesome his family are. They think Flora set fire to Mrs Doriot-Buffet's hedge on purpose.

Jas said thank you, but she would rather stay at home.

Pixie has gone away for the weekend, and Mum and Dad were invited to a party. I said I would stay at home with Jas and Pumpkin.

'But the fireworks!' Flora said.

'We can watch them from the roof.'

At first, after we made up, I thought that everything with Dodi was back to normal. And it is – sort of. It's just that now she has decided she is so in love with Jake, neither of them have time for the rest of us any more. I spoke to Grandma this morning, and she said all actions have consequences and I should have thought about that when I told Dodi to be truthful with Jake, but I honestly don't know how I could have foreseen that Dodi telling Jake he got on her nerves would lead to the Great Romance of the Century.

Other consequences of Dodi and Jake are that Tom has been so inspired by them he has decided he is in love with Hattie, and that Colin has gone off in disgust to hang out with some of the other boys in our year. And the overwhelming consequence is that I have no-one to go to the fireworks with.

The house was very quiet after the others had gone.

'What shall we do?' I asked.

Jas said she didn't want to do anything. Then the house phone rang, and it was Todd asking to speak to Jas because he didn't have anyone to go to the park with either.

'Tell him to go away,' Jas said.

'But he's your friend!'

'I don't have any friends.'

Apart from the one after Iris died, it was the most miserable Bonfire Night I have ever had. Jas and I went to the shops and I tried to buy sparklers, but they told me I was too young. We walked back past Marek's house, on the other side of the square, but all the lights were out again, even the one on the top floor.

Back home, I made hot chocolate, and then we wrapped up in duvets and went out on to the flat roof outside my bedroom window to watch the display, but there were too many trees and buildings in the way. In the distance, you could hear the music from the park, and all the bangs, and the air was full of the smell of gunpowder and smoke, but the only fireworks you could actually see were the really high ones, and I felt stupid because I was wearing Flora's bunny onesie and Pixie's tiara to try and cheer Jas up, but she just wore an old grey jumper of Twig's over a pair of grubby leggings and only smiled once, when a pink rocket exploded right above our heads and burst into a thousand silver stars.

Twig and Flora came back together about half an hour ago, raving about how spectacular the fireworks were. I can hear Flora now in her bedroom, talking on her phone. I'm sitting out on my roof again. All around me, the night is still full of explosions. Another rocket burst above me, blue this time, filled with golden spirals that fizzed then faded into the smoke, and I thought that firework is doing the same thing Marek does. It won't last long, but for the time it's burning up there, we are all watching it, and maybe that is why Marek draws in the street, why Zoran makes music and Flora acts and Jas and

Nancy Chikado write poetry, and I want to make films – so people can see us.

I wonder where Marek watched the fireworks from. I can't imagine him in the park with everyone else, crowded on the muddy lawn, the gaudy lights of the funfair, the blast of the sound system. Maybe he went out on the streets, taking advantage of the fact that everyone else was staring at the sky, to draw another picture. Maybe he is working hard with a box of chalks, decorating a pavement, a wall, the side of a building with his own multi-coloured starbursts.

I wonder what that would look like – the fireworks in Marek's head.

Monday 8 November

He wasn't in school today. It took me ages to work up the courage to do it, but this afternoon I went to his house.

Marek's house is different from ours. Our front garden is a mess, with weeds growing wherever the ground isn't covered with ivy and a mass of dead roses that nobody has bothered to cut since the summer. The paint on the windows is flaking, and the front door is scuffed from where people kick it open when they come in with bikes and buggies and shopping. The paint on Marek's house gleams. There are window boxes with plants clipped into perfect spheres. The front garden is paved, with olive trees growing in tubs. Even the letterbox looks expensive.

I will just say I came to check he is OK, I thought. In my school bag, I had a new worksheet for *Of Mice and Men*. I will just say I brought English homework.

I steeled myself and reached for the bell, but before I even touched it the front door flew open and I jumped about a mile into the air.

'Quick,' Marek hissed. 'In case she sees you.'

Without thinking, I darted forward. He reached out and pulled me in. I did think, even then, that he might be mad.

'Who?' I asked.

'Violet!'

'Um . . .'

'Mrs Doriot-Buffet. Our neighbour? Your sister set fire to her hedge. Quickly!'

The inside of Marek's house is exactly what you would expect from the outside. Marble tiles in the hall. Shiny honey-coloured wood in the living room. The curtains are made of silk, the sofas are pale and unstained, the chairs are velvet and uncomfortable, all the books on the shelves are bound in leather. The chimney surround is decorated with carvings of ladies in flowing dresses carrying baskets of fruit, and in the middle of the mantelpiece there is a china lady with very big lilac skirts and a pineapple head. I mean, literally. Her head is fruit.

'Tata gave her to Mum for her birthday,' Marek said, following my gaze. 'She's very expensive. I think it's meant to be art.'

'Right,' I said.

We stood around for a bit. I don't think I have ever felt more awkward.

'You weren't in school,' I started saying, at the same time as he said, with his funny half smile, 'She thinks your family is out of control.'

'Sorry, who thinks that?'

'Mrs Doriot-Buffet. Because of the fire. Look, my parents will be home soon. We've been away, they just went to the shops . . .'

And then there was the sound of a key in the front door, and it was opening, and a woman's voice was calling, 'Marek, where are you?'

Marek hesitated. Then another voice piped up – Mr Valenta.

'Where is the boy? Where has he got to?'

Marek hissed, 'Hide!' and pushed me to the floor behind a sofa.

The Valentas argue differently to us. At home, people shout a lot and storm about slamming doors and saying things like they are going to run away because no-one understands them, but it never lasts very long and no-one ever holds a grudge. At the Valentas', it feels more serious.

There wasn't a lot of room behind the sofa. It stood in a big bay in front of the window, and I guess that despite their perfect house the Valentas aren't any better at housework than anybody else, because the floor was very dusty. I wriggled around to try and find a comfortable position that also didn't make me stick out, being very careful how I breathed so I didn't cough and sneeze. Really it's a miracle that no-one heard me, but I guess that's because they were all too busy being angry.

It didn't start with shouting. In fact, when Mr Valenta came into the room, I could tell he was in an excellent mood again.

'Good news!' he cried, and I could just picture him rubbing his hands as he spoke. 'I have just taken a telephone call from St Llwydian. They have offered you a place!'

Marek said, 'Oh,' and the way he said it I imagined him with all the air suddenly squashed out of him, like a cushion when you sit on it, or your tummy when you're punched.

'Oh? Oh! Is that all you have to say? One of the best schools in the country, and "Oh"? Why are you not delighted?'

Mrs Valenta murmured, 'Stefan, please, not again.'

Marek mumbled something that sounded like 'You know why.'

'This is a magnificent opportunity!' Mr Valenta's voice was rising. 'Do you imagine that I ever had such an opportunity when I was growing up?'

'Stefan ...' Once again Mrs Valenta tried to calm her husband. Once again, he ignored her.

'Presidents and ministers send their sons to this school! Heads of business! Royalty! Do you think I was offered the chance to rub shoulders with the sons of millionaires and princes? Not I! I began to work when I was fourteen years old!'

'But I don't care about any of that!' Marek protested.

'Look at this house! Do you think we could live here if I were a violinist? That your mother could wear silk dresses, that we would drive a big fine car? Ski in Zermatt, holiday on the Côte d'Azur? Do you? Do you?'

'Why won't you listen to me?' Marek yelled, and there was an edge to his voice I've never heard from anyone at home – desperate and angry.

'Because you do not make sense!'

A door slammed. Mr Valenta bellowed, 'Marek! Marek, I only want what is best for you!'

'No you don't!' Marek's voice sounded far away – upstairs, I think. 'You want what is best for you!'

Don't leave me alone, I panicked, but maybe Marek was actually helping, because then there were more footsteps as Mr Valenta stormed out of the room after him.

I should never have come. I was shaking as I prepared to creep out of my hiding place. Just a few steps across the hall.

And then I froze at the sound of high heels tapping on wood, coming towards me.

'You can come out now.'

Mrs Valenta's elegant face appeared over the top of the sofa.

'I…'

'Shhh.' She put a finger to her lips, and nodded towards the door.

I crept out from behind the sofa, tiptoed across the honey parquet and the marble hall and fled.

*

At home, Dad and Jas were sitting together in the armchair in the study, watching Flora do a sort of moon walk. I squeezed in on the arm next to them.

'What is she doing?' I asked.

Flora did what looked like a slow motion front crawl with her arms, raised her leg with surprising elegance almost to her shoulder, wobbled like she was falling backwards, righted herself with no apparent effort and resumed her swimming while shaking her head with a finger pressed to her mouth.

'She can't talk, because sound doesn't travel in space.' Jas looked mesmerised.

'But why is she in space?'

'She's rehearsing her play.' Dad was watching Flora with a mixture of bafflement and delight.

Flora flipped on her back and waved her arms and legs in the air.

'I thought the play was *Romeo and Juliet*?'

'Angel has decided to set it in space.'

'Why?'

Flora sat up, back on planet Earth.

'Because space is a giant metaphor for human alienation. It's like, Romeo and Juliet are trying to reach each other, but the universe is between them.'

'But how are you going to talk if sound doesn't travel?'

'We'll be in space crafts, obviously. Romeo and Juliet each have their own spaceship, and they have to spacewalk between the two. The bit I just played is actually right after I kill myself. It's super-powerful.'

'I don't understand either,' Jas whispered to me.

'That,' Flora said, 'is because you are very young. When you are older, you will appreciate Angel's genius.'

She swept out of the room. Dad and Jas and I burst out laughing, but I couldn't stop my mind from thinking.

Marek shoved me behind a sofa. A sofa!

Imagine being so afraid of your parents you didn't want to be caught with a friend. Maybe it's because I'm a girl? Or because of Flora, and the fire? I felt sorry for him, for the argument with his father and the school in Wales he doesn't want to go to, but mainly I felt humiliated.

If you had to pick somewhere that was the exact opposite of the Valentas' living room, it would be Dad's study. Some people (like me) can't work unless everything around them is absolutely tidy. Dad can't work unless he is surrounded by absolute chaos. There are towers of books stacked on the floor all around his study with dust bunnies swirling around their bases, and you can't actually see an inch of desk for all the papers that cover it, with his laptop balanced on top. His bookcases are so full it looks like the books might burst off the shelves at any minute, and the armchair is a disaster: it's missing one leg, which Dad has replaced with a stack of dictionaries, and the back cushion doesn't match the seat, and it has orange stuffing spilling out of the side where Twig once accidentally stabbed it with a pair of scissors.

'Do you think we're out of control?' I asked Dad. 'I mean, as a family?'

Dad said he didn't even understand the question.

'Look around you,' I said.

Dad looked at his study like he was seeing it for the first time. 'Do you mean this room?' he asked. 'Do you think it's messy?'

'It looks like a bomb exploded in it.'

'I suppose it does.' He rubbed his eyes. 'Do you think I should tidy it?'

I snuggled into his shoulder. He was wearing the same cardigan he had worn when the Valentas came round, his favourite with the holes at the elbows.

'No,' I said. 'I think you should keep it exactly as it is.'

It is very difficult to know what to say to a person when you have not only recently discovered he is a brilliant secret street artist, but also overheard him have a screaming row with his father while you hid behind his sofa. I think Marek felt the same because in school today we completely ignored each other until English, when Dodi passed me a note from him.

'What does it say?' she whispered.

I didn't want to laugh. I was still cross about the sofa. But when I looked at the note, I almost laughed out loud, because he had drawn it – the sofa, I mean, and my head poking out of the side, and underneath he'd written 'I am so, so sorry' and . . .

'Blue!' Dodi hissed.

'He wants to meet me after school,' I whispered.

'Oh my God! Will you go?'

'I don't know.'

I didn't reply to the note. I do have my pride.

But I did meet him after school.

We took the Tube into town, but Marek didn't tell me where we were going. On the train, we talked about Miss Foundry, *Of Mice and Men*, skateboards, and the beautiful architecture of Prague. We didn't talk about secret chalk drawings, boarding schools in Wales, shouty parents or sofas.

We changed trains at Tottenham Court Road and finally got off at Charing Cross.

The other night, when we went to the theatre, London was all bright lights and traffic and people and noise. Today, just after four o'clock in the afternoon, it was completely different. The sun was going down and the sky was pink and blue like in Devon, and the winter light was soft and clear but sort of shimmering too, and it made it feel like we were in a film or something, and the tall buildings along the Strand, Trafalgar Square and the lions and Nelson's Column and the big arch and Whitehall were all part of a giant, exciting, wonderful set.

There was a street performer singing and that made it feel unreal too, like it was the music to the film, and all the business people rushing and the tourists milling and the old people sitting about were like extras in a weird story where Marek and I were playing the leads.

It was beautiful.

'Blue?'

Marek's voice brought me back to earth. We were standing in the middle of Trafalgar Square, with Whitehall behind us. He pointed straight ahead.

'The National Gallery?'

Marek nodded.

Museums and art galleries are only ever things we do with Dad, who drags us round making us read every label and saying things like, 'Look, children! This is a perfect example of . . .' neo-gothic-classical-something or other none of us understands. Marek is the complete opposite. We swept through the gallery like the paintings on the walls were nothing more than the pictures we did when we were little that Mum used to stick on the fridge, until we finally stopped and Marek said, 'Look!'

The painting he chose was quite surprising. We passed lots of others that were way more interesting. There was a huge one of a woman about to have her head chopped off that was horrible but beautiful too, in a terrifying way, and there were lots of saints being tortured and ships tossed about on stormy seas and half-naked people dancing, but Marek's painting didn't even look like it was finished. In fact, it wasn't even a painting, more like a rough brownish drawing of two women sitting close together with babies on their laps.

We sat on a bench and looked at it.

'This is my favourite thing in the whole of London,' Marek said.

I looked closer. I could see that it was good. I mean, you don't get a picture in the National Gallery if you're not good. It was done by Leonardo da Vinci around 1499. The women (who were the Virgin Mary and her cousin) and the babies (Jesus and his cousin John the Baptist) were beautiful, and if you looked for long enough it was almost like they were alive. But still . . .

'Why this one?' I asked.

'Because it's perfect,' Marek said.

Marek knows a lot about Leonardo da Vinci, who wasn't just a painter but also a sculptor and a mathematician and an architect and an engineer. He designed flying machines and he painted the Mona Lisa, which is probably the most famous painting in the world, and one day Marek wants to be just like him.

'Which bit?' I asked, feeling dizzy.

Marek said, very seriously, 'I want to make something so good it lasts for ever.'

Something happened to Marek in the gallery. His coat was bunched under his arm, and his shirt was untucked, with the sleeves pushed up past his elbows. The laces of one of his expensive leather shoes were undone, and his hair stood up in all directions because he has a habit, when he is looking at pictures, of running his hands through it. He looked almost like a normal boy. Actually, he looked better than a normal boy. Scruffed up, Marek is disconcertingly handsome.

We went to the café and bought tea in takeaway cups that we took outside to drink on the steps and there at last, in the dark in the middle of Trafalgar Square, Marek began to explain. He was so, so sorry about the sofa, he said again. It was like I thought – Flora, and the fire, and our out-of-control family. 'I couldn't risk upsetting Tata,' he said. 'We'd just been to see that stupid school in Wales, they had this open day ... We were away all weekend. I think he thought it would impress me.'

'That sounds ... nice,' I said. Marek scowled and said it wasn't, it was horrible, and the last thing he wanted to do was go to boarding school in the middle of nowhere.

'I'm just getting used to London,' he said. Our eyes met for a second, and then we both looked away and stared at our feet.

'I guess you want to know about the drawings,' he mumbled, and I whispered that yes, sort of, I mean if he didn't mind.

'Tata doesn't like me drawing,' he said. 'He was really proud when I was a younger because I was better than everyone else – that's not me showing off, it's just true. But then last year my art teacher told my parents he thought I had a real gift, and I should seriously consider going to art college after school, and he suddenly went all weird.'

'Weird?'

'Art is not serious!' Marek said, imitating Mr Valenta. 'You must concentrate on proper subjects that will make you good at business! Do you know why we came to London?'

I tried to remember. 'Something about your father's business?'

'Tata wants to expand it. He says he's doing it for me – so after I've finished school, and whatever business degree he wants me to do, I can work with him.'

'Oh,' I said. I tried to imagine Marek in a business suit. It should have been easy, given the clothes he usually wears, but all I could see was Marek in the alleyway near the theatre with a chalk in his hand.

'You can see how wrong that would be, can't you?' Marek insisted.

'Yes,' I said. 'I can.'

'Mum says it's because of what happened to him, because he couldn't study music. She says it was a huge sacrifice for him, and he has to prove it was worth it by always providing the best for us. But if music was such a sacrifice for him, he'd let me go to art college, don't you think? He knows what art means to me. It's like ... it's like breathing. It's like air. But he won't even let me take Art GCSE.'

Marek gazed at me, like he was begging me to agree with him, and I didn't know what to say, because I don't think I've ever heard anyone be quite so passionate about anything, and also because I still had so many questions about, well, about me. I glanced at my phone, and saw that I had a load of messages from Pixie and Dodi, asking where I was.

'I have to go,' I said.

We didn't go back the way we came. Instead, when we got to Charing Cross, Marek led me down a cobbled street towards Embankment. Then, when I made to go into the station, he took my arm and pulled me on towards the river.

'Just a few minutes,' he said.

We climbed up the steps on to the railway bridge and leaned on the railings, looking east along the Thames, and it was like we were looking at two Londons, because St Paul's and the South Bank theatres and the embankment were all lit up and reflected in the dark, almost black water.

'It's not as pretty as Prague,' he said. 'But it's not bad.'

'About the drawings . . .'

'He won't let me draw at home,' Marek said quickly. 'And he made me leave Prague. The drawings, they're like revenge, you know? Like I draw in secret, but where everyone can see me.'

I didn't say anything to that, because I'm not sure it's a proper revenge when the person you are being revengeful towards doesn't know that you're doing it.

'They're like my way of claiming London,' Marek ploughed on. 'Like I'm making it mine.'

The things we weren't saying hung between us, so thick I felt I could touch them.

The zebra.

The bluebells.

The ponies.

'Marek . . .'

'Do you know the first time I saw you?' he interrupted.

'That day with the dachshund,' I said. 'You'd been playing tennis with your dad.'

'That was the second time. The first time, you didn't even know I was there. I'd been in London for a week, and I was furious with Tata for bringing me here. I went out to draw in the garden in the square, and there you were, lying on the grass with your camera. I looked to see what you were filming and it was just a cat, staring at the ground. I couldn't understand why you thought it was interesting. And then suddenly the cat pounced on something, and started going crazy, trying to catch a mouse or something, I guess, and I thought ... it sounds stupid.'

'What?' I asked.

'I thought you were an artist. Because that is what artists do, isn't it? They watch. They see things differently. They try to show things differently.'

He ran his hands through his hair again. He was actually beginning to look less like a normal boy, and more and more like a mad person.

'Don't you think?' he asked.

'Yes,' I said. 'I do.'

'Violet told us who you were, your names and everything. Bluebell. I liked that so much. And I guess ... what I'm trying to say is ... the drawings. They're not just about Dad. I sort of did them ... what I mean is, they were for you too. Sort of ... one artist to another. To ... to introduce myself, I guess ... I put them where I thought you might see them, so you could see the real me, because at school ... and that terrible drink at your house ... because usually, I am trying to please Tata, you know ... so he won't have an excuse to send me away . . . Because part of why I don't want to go away is . . . well, a lot of it is because of you.'

'Me?'

Even in the dark, I could see that Marek was almost as red as I was.

'You know, you could have just talked to me,' I murmured.

'I didn't know what to say! I'm rubbish at words – I'm much better with pictures.' He swallowed, stared down at the river. 'I really like you, Blue.'

Our hands were resting next to each other on the bridge's parapet. I slid mine towards his, so close they were almost touching.

'Your drawings . . .' I said. 'They make me see things I never saw before. They make me want to be a better artist myself.'

He smiled properly then, the first time ever since I met him, and it was just . . . lovely.

He tucked his shirt in on the Tube home, smoothed back his hair, wrapped his cashmere scarf carefully around his neck. By the time we came out, he looked exactly like he does every day at school, but as we parted on the Avenue he pressed a piece of paper in my hand. 'My email address,' he said. 'Will you send me some of your films? It's only fair, since you've seen all my drawings.'

And then he kissed me. Just a tiny kiss, on the cheek. But enough to turn my legs to jelly.

Wednesday 10 November

Dodi messaged me approximately once every three minutes all evening yesterday, but I never answered her and when she finally called the house phone, I got Jas to tell her I was in the bath.

'With her head under water,' Jas said. 'So she can't talk.'

The gallery, the steps, the bridge, everything we talked about. Marek's kiss. They're like this huge wonderful secret I don't want to share with a single person.

'Where did you go?' Dodi asked this morning when we met on the way to school. 'What did you do, what did you say and did he try to kiss you?'

'We just went for a walk,' I said.

'Another walk!'

'He needed help with his English homework. It wasn't a big deal.'

If I told Dodi my secret, it would spoil it. She wouldn't understand, about going to galleries or looking at the Thames, or almost but not quite touching hands, or smiles so bright they were dazzling. She would want details of the kiss, and be disappointed it was so quick that afterwards, when I got home, I wondered if it had actually happened.

Marek and I didn't talk today, but all the time at school I felt my skin prickling, knowing that he was near and once, when we passed in the corridor, we half-smiled at each other and I thought I would burn up from blushing.

I don't think we're going out now. I mean, he hasn't asked me. And when he kissed me, it wasn't a ... well, it wasn't a boyfriend kiss. And I'm fine with just friends, I honestly am. I think.

'Send me one of your videos,' he said, but I can't – can I?

What he says about me being an artist, it's sweet but it's not true – is it? I thought of Peter, saying 'Your camera will turn it into a work of beauty' and 'One day you'll make history'.

Will turn into. One day. In the future.

Not now. Absolutely not now at all.

*

When I got home from school, Pumpkin was spitting mashed carrots out at Pixie who was in full army fatigues, and the part of the kitchen table not splattered with his supper was covered in A3 sheets of drawing paper splodged all over with angry dabs of paint, with Jas standing at the head of the table jabbing at a fresh sheet and complaining loudly that it was no good, no good at all.

'The despair of the artist at work,' Pixie informed me as I came in. 'She seeks the Muse, but the Muse eludes her.'

'Stupid art project!' Jas was flicking globs of red paint now. Some of it landed in Pumpkin's supper. Quite a lot hit Pixie and also the table and the floor. A few specks landed on the paper.

'So now you *are* doing the art project?' I said.

'Mr Boniface says I have to. He says I'm very creative. He says if I don't, he'll be so disappointed.'

She swept her arm across the page to her brow, in imitation of Mr Boniface's disappointment. A jam jar full of red water and paintbrushes crashed to the floor. Pumpkin started to cry.

'I can't paint!' Jas wailed. 'I can't draw! I thought flowers would be easy!'

Twig came in wearing shorts and running shoes, red and sweating and looking like he was going to throw up.

'What's wrong with you?' I asked.

Twig gasped a lot and said it was all part of rugby training, and Coach had said he needed to do more running because he's too slow compared to the others.

At that Welsh school, they do ten miles before breakfast, I thought.

Twig staggered over to look at Jas's drawing.

'What are those supposed to be?' Twig asked.

'They're GERANIUMS,' Jas howled.

'And they're wonderful!' Pixie cried. 'So red! So colourful! So very like geraniums!'

'I thought she was doing a poem,' Twig said.

'Mr Boniface says it doesn't count,' Pixie said. 'He says poetry is not art, and she has to do a painting.'

Marek could help Jas, I thought, and then I thought, I really am obsessed.

Flora's play opens tomorrow. That will take my mind off Marek. Dad has invited everyone, even though she keeps trying to stop him. Zoran is coming from Devon with Grandma and Skye and his parents. She says she doesn't want anyone who knows her to go in case we put her off, but I don't think she means it, because she never stops talking about it. And anyway, as Dad says, what use is a play if it doesn't have an audience?

It's like Marek. What is the point of painting if people don't know it's him?

Does Marek regret what he told me the other

night? Is that why he isn't speaking to me? I wonder what he would think of Flora's play. We're having a big dinner, all of us, the night before – should I invite him? Would he come? If he did, would he have to come in disguise so his father didn't know he was hanging out with out-of-control pyromaniacs?

Oh God, I have got to stop.

The Film Diaries of Bluebell Gadsby

Scene Ten
A Party in Chatsworth Square

Evening, inside the Gadsby kitchen. The table and work surfaces groan with food. On the stove sits a huge vegetarian casserole made by PIXIE. On the table sit the rice and chutneys to eat with it, together with MOTHER's salads (green, mixed leaves) and the cakes brought by LIZZIE (Skye's mother) and GRANDMA – brownies, shortbread, rhubarb crumble and gingerbread. In the garden, despite the cold, FATHER is firing up a barbecue with ISAMBARD HANRATTY on which to cook the sausages and potatoes brought from Devon by ZORAN. TWIG is showing SKYE a beetle he discovered yesterday in the garden. JAS, still spattered with red paint, sits on the swing reciting poetry to PUMPKIN in his buggy, who joins in with the occasional loud squawk.

The doorbell rings and MAUD, PETER and BARNEY appear, bearing an entire salmon as a gift. Maud wears a long white nightdress over a polo-neck jumper, thick tights and leather boots. Her hair is done up in ringlets.

MOTHER
Goodness, more people!

MAUD
Didn't Flora tell you? She's invited us to stay.

Mother says no, Flora didn't tell her, and why is Maud dressed like that. Maud explains that she is performing Wendy Darling in the drama school's *Peter Pan*. Father cries, the more the merrier! And the salmon gets thrown on to the barbecue to burn along with the sausages.

Later, FLORA arrives back from her dress rehearsal. Barney seizes his fiddle and accompanies her into the garden. Maud goes one better and gets out her trumpet. Zoran (who is a little drunk) picks up the melody on the piano. And now the party is in full swing.

Lizzie Hanratty, Mother and Pixie start to dance. Twig grabs Pumpkin's tambourine. Pumpkin howls. The musicians all start playing their own variations on Barney's melody. Zoran continues to thump away at the piano, while the portable instruments parade from the garden through the house, and spill into the street where the dancers twirl, laughing, in the front garden. Barney's fiddle goes faster and faster. Maud, not to be outdone, leaps onto the garden wall.

A car drives past, slowly and for CAMERAMAN (BLUEBELL) – time stops. Maud, on the wall. The breeze lifting her ringlets, her nightdress billowing behind her, the trees and gardens of Chatsworth Square in shadow behind her as she, only she, is caught in the car's headlights with her trumpet raised to her lips. An angel in Doc Marten boots. Human, and superhuman. A creature of heaven risen from the streets.

She is a work of beauty.

But a figure is marching towards them. The figure is Mrs Henderson, and she is not amused by people playing trumpets and fiddles and guitars and tambourines under her window at ten o'clock at night.

She is not interested in angels, however beautiful.

Maud jumps down from her wall. The party disbands. Only Barney is left with his fiddle. He is lost to the tune he is playing and cannot leave until it is finished. Cameraman grows aware that the car is still there, the one which caught Maud in its headlights.

It is a massive black four-by-four, and its driver is Mr Valenta. Cameraman expects to see anger, or outrage. Instead, all she can think as she looks at him is that she never saw anyone look so sad.

The music stops. The car drives away. The last of the party goes inside.

Skye just leaned over my shoulder and asked, 'What are you doing?'

The house is full to bursting, with people sleeping on every sofa and blow-up mattress we can find. Skye and I are sharing with Twig and Jas.

'She's doing what she always does before bed,' Twig said. 'Scribble, scribble, scribble.'

I closed my diary.

'I'm writing down my film of the party.'

'Can I see it?' Skye asked. 'The film, I mean, not your diary.'

I hesitated. Then, feeling very brave, I handed over my camera. They are all piled on Skye's mattress now, watching the film as I write, all laughing and, 'Is that really what I look like?' and commenting on the music and the singing. Any second now they'll get to the bit with Maud.

They won't notice. Of course they won't notice. I mean, they won't think it's that good.

But there's silence from the mattress on the floor. Silence except for the clear notes of a trumpet.

Then Skye said, 'Blue, that was amazing.'

'You made Maud look like an angel,' Jas said.

Skye gave me back the camera. He took off his

glasses and peered at me, and it was like he was seeing me properly for the first time. 'You'll win an Oscar one day, Blue.'

'Flora's the one who's going to win an Oscar,' I said, but I hid my face so they wouldn't see how pleased I was.

I did it, I did it, I did it! I thought, as they continued to exclaim over my video. Me! Me! I made something amazing!

Everyone is asleep now and the house is quiet. I'm sitting on the landing so as not to disturb the others. I've loaded the film onto my laptop, and in my hand I'm holding the scrap of paper Marek gave me with his email address. '*Send me one of your videos ...*' Can I? Do I dare?

What if he doesn't understand it? What if all he sees is a girl playing the trumpet?

Flora just got up to go to the bathroom, and came to sit with me a while.

'I'm scared,' she said.

'For tomorrow?'

'What if I'm not good enough?'

And I don't know what to think about anything now, if even Flora thinks she isn't good enough.

Quickly, without thinking about it, I opened up email, typed Marek's address into the destination box, attached my file and pressed Send.

The Film Diaries of Bluebell Gadsby

Scene Eleven
A Brief Description of
Romeo And Juliet (In Space)
by William Shakespeare,
Adapted and Directed by
Angel De Castro and Starring
Miss Flora Gadsby as Juliet

A small theatre, painted black. A stage about the size of the Gadsby kitchen. Thirty rows of benches seating fifteen people each, of which about half are occupied, though audience consists almost entirely of friends and family of the cast, as well as two perplexed Japanese tourists and several journalists. The GADSBY FAMILY PARTY occupies all of the fourth row. The adults sit at one end, then SKYE, JASMINE, CAMERAMAN (BLUEBELL) and TWIG, with the DRAMA STUDENTS on the other side.

The set is divided into three parts. On the left is Romeo's spaceship, with furniture painted metallic gold and actors all dressed in yellow.

On the right is Juliet's spaceship, with furniture all painted metallic silver, and actors all dressed in grey. The middle section between the spaceships – outer space – has a backdrop of twinkling stars which are actually lots of strings of fairy lights. Inside the spaceships, the actors move about like they're on Earth, but whenever they go into outer space, they have to pretend to float because they are in zero gravity.

They use lightsabres for the sword fights.

JASMINE
(about two minutes in)
I don't understand.

CAMERAMAN
They're in space.

JASMINE

I mean I don't understand what
they're saying.

CAMERAMAN

That's because it was written four
hundred years ago.

TWIG

If it was written four hundred years
ago, how come they're in space?

JASMINE

And how long is it going to last?

Skye puts his hand over her mouth to
get her to shut up. Jasmine snorts
with laughter. Snot shoots out of her
nose on to Skye's hand. Twig says she's
disgusting. Jasmine giggles so hard
she starts to hiccough. Camera jiggles
as Skye hides his face in Cameraman's
shoulder to stifle his own laughter.

ALL OF THE ADULTS, PLUS SOME OTHER
MEMBERS OF THE AUDIENCE
Shhhhhhhh!!!!

I don't know exactly what I was expecting from Flora's play.

The only time I have seen *Romeo and Juliet* before was the film with Leonardo DiCaprio and Claire Danes, and I'm not sure it's fair to compare it to what we saw tonight. A big Hollywood movie with world-famous actors is not the same thing at all as a play staged in a tiny theatre above a pub where downstairs people are watching football on telly and you know whenever anybody scores because you can hear the cheers, and it smells of beer and chips and the landlord comes in halfway through a lightsabre fight to say, 'Remind me what time you lot finish in here?' then gets cross because people tell him to hush.

But still, I think I was expecting something grander.

Also, I don't think *Romeo and Juliet* works when it's set in outer space. Maybe if the theatre was bigger, and there were proper special effects, like spaceships that actually look like spaceships instead of someone's furniture sprayed with bicycle paint, and proper uniforms like on *Star Trek*, and laser beams for the sword fights.

Maybe.

Even then, I don't think I see the point. Like for the balcony scene, when Juliet comes out and starts to go on about how much she loves Romeo, and he climbs up and says how much he loves her too. In the film, that is a very romantic scene, and then it becomes funny and sweet as well because they both jump into a swimming pool and it makes you laugh but really you're wishing that Leonardo DiCaprio would climb up to your window and jump into a swimming pool for you.

It's just not the same when Romeo is wearing yellow tights and waving his legs about like he's about to get sucked into a space vortex.

It was bad.

So bad the Japanese tourists and a couple of the journalists and even some of the relatives left at the interval, and when we all went down to the pub everyone spent ages choosing what sort of crisps and drinks they wanted and *Romeo and Juliet* (in Space) was like a giant white elephant in the room that nobody wanted to talk about.

The second half was even more awful, right up to the end when Juliet kills herself after finding Romeo dead and drags him out of the spaceship and the two of them spacewalk away together and she dies because she can't breathe but they're joined together for ever by the bonds of love, except he lets go and floats away and it's Leonardo DiCaprio all over again except now it's *Titanic* but considerably less tragic because he's wearing yellow tights.

There was a long silence as the actors lined up to take their bow, like the audience had no idea how to react. Then Dad got to his feet and started to cheer, then Zoran, and Skye dragged me up too and soon the entire audience of friends and family were standing and whooping, and it was worth sitting through the whole awful thing just for Flora's happy, shining face.

'Did you like it?' she asked afterwards. She was glowing and she couldn't keep still, but kept on hugging everybody.

Peter and Maud (still in her nightie) and Barney, who are all very good actors, were all 'Darling you were magnificent,' and Mum and Dad were all, 'We're so proud of you,' but it was a lot more difficult for the rest of us.

'It was mad,' Skye said.

'Spacey,' Twig offered.

'I didn't understand a single thing,' said Jas.

'Blue?'

'It was different,' I said, and it shows how happy Flora is that she took these all as compliments.

Marek hasn't answered my email. I've checked about a hundred times, and it did send, and there's no notification saying it was the wrong address. Maybe he's one of those people who never actually checks their inbox. But then if he was, why would he give me his email?

He doesn't like it. That must be the thing. He doesn't like it, and he doesn't know how to tell me, and I don't know which is worse. Him not liking it, or him being embarrassed about not liking it.

Oh God, how am I going to talk to him? Even look at him? Even be in the same classroom?

Maybe it will be all right. Maybe his dad will force him to go to St Llwydian and I will never have to see him again.

But then that would be so sad . . .

I am going to throw my phone away. No, I need it . . . I am going to wrap it up in a towel, and stuff it in a plastic bag, and bury the plastic bag in the garden until the end of the weekend. That way, I won't be tempted to look at it again.

He still hasn't replied to me.

Maybe my video isn't good at all, and the others were all just being kind.

Maybe I will never have a film premiere in an Imax cinema, or make an Oscar acceptance speech, or walk down a red carpet. My life will never be a Hollywood movie, and I will never wear glittering dresses but spend the rest of my days wrapped in old brown cardigans thrown out by my little sister.

Maybe Marek is horrifically embarrassed and doesn't know how to tell me he hates it.

Sunday 14 November

All the others left this morning, back to Scotland and Devon. Then, at about half-past three this afternoon, the house started to shake as Flora stormed down the stairs, shouting.

'I hate journalists!' Flora cried. 'And reviewers! And critics! And the whole stupid internet!'

The house shook again as she slammed the front door.

We all looked up Flora's reviews. It didn't take long, because there weren't many of them, and most were very short. 'Absurd' was the word that came up the most. Also, 'preposterous', 'ridiculous' and in one case, 'a complete waste of an evening'. There were a few lines about Angel. One reviewer, who was nicer than most, said she thought it was possible he might one day do something interesting because he obviously has a lot of imagination, and she also said that Flora was, 'Not bad given the challenges of the production' – meaning, I suppose, exactly what I wrote about the play: that it's very difficult to look tragic and romantic when you're also pretending to be swimming about in space.

Nobody else mentioned Flora at all, unless you count the review that said, 'Every single aspect of this production was awful'.

Grown-up theatre critics are as mean as primary school cupcake girls.

I don't think the show has sold many tickets. Twig went on the ticket-selling website and pretended to do a group booking for thirty people all wanting to sit together, and it wasn't a problem at all.

Flora came back still in a temper and spent most of the evening in her room. Mum tried to talk to her, but Flora just told her to go away. Dad says that tomorrow he is going to call her drama school and convince them to take her back. He says the show probably won't last its run and if Ms Foulkes-Watson will have her she can go back before Christmas.

Skye made Peter and Maud look at my film before they left. Maud loved it. She says she's never going to take her nightdress off, and go about all the time leaping on walls to play the trumpet. Peter told her that one day I was going to make a film with them all in it, and she said, 'Yes please!' and also, 'We'll all be famous if you make us look like that.' Peter said again about applying for that film course next summer.

I feel a little better about my lack of talent.

But there is still no news from Marek.

Monday 15 November

I didn't have my camera with me this morning on the way to school, but if I had, and I'd decided to film, it would have looked something like this.

Scene Twelve
The Angel on the Bridge

Monday morning and Blenheim Avenue is the usual bustle of pedestrians, pushchairs, office workers, school kids, cars, buses, cyclists etc., but something is different today.

A crowd has gathered at the pedestrian crossing by the bus stop, the crossing CAMERAMAN (BLUEBELL), DODI, TWIG and JASMINE use every single morning on their way to school. There is a wall opposite the crossing. A plain, twelve-foot wall made of London brick, the side of someone's house, of no interest whatsoever.

And yet all these people are looking at it.

> TWIG
> It must be another one of those drawings.

> JASMINE
> I want to see!

> CAMERAMAN
> (suddenly feeling flustered, because, people looking at walls? This can only mean one thing)
> You'll be late. We should go. It's probably nothing.

> DODI
> I'm going to look.

Cameraman follows Dodi as she starts to push her way through the crowd, picking up snatches of conversation – 'There's St Paul's!' and, 'There's even a boat on the river' and, 'Look at the reflection in the water'.

And Cameraman knows, before she even sees it, what the drawing will be.

The river at night, the embankment, the theatres on the South Bank. Two solitary figures on Hungerford Bridge, their hands on the railings, looking down at the water.

Exactly as it was.

No, not exactly.

Because this time their hands are touching.

And in the star-strung sky above them, an angel watches. An angel wearing a nightdress over leather boots and a jumper, with a trumpet raised to her lips.

That is what it was like this morning on the way to school.

He's better with pictures. Didn't he tell me that himself?

And that picture … Those hands, touching! And the angel …

'It's Maud!' said Jas. 'It's that video you took of her!'

'Don't be silly!' I blushed. 'It could be any old angel.'

'And the girl …' Dodi peered at her. 'She looks like you.'

'Just because she's got plaits and glasses!' I cried. 'She could be anyone!'

They all stared. I marched away before they could see my huge, silly, delighted grin.

He liked it! That was all I could think. He liked it, and he likes me!

My heart thumped and thundered in my chest all the way to school. I'm surprised the others couldn't hear it, or that they didn't ask me if I was ill because I felt so sick. My mouth felt dry as sand as I walked in the school gates, and I honestly think if someone had spoken to me at that moment I wouldn't have heard them, because the world felt like it does when you have a cold – woolly and distant and like you and it are in completely different places – and all I could think, along with he liked it he liked it he liked it was what do I say what do I say what do I say?

But he wasn't there.

I checked my phone after first period. There was no message from him. I checked again after second and third period, during morning break and during Maths. Still no message. At lunchtime, I realised that he doesn't have my phone number, only an email address. There's no Wi-Fi at school, so I went to the library and checked my emails. Nothing. I opened a new email box, typed 'Hope you're OK, I loved the drawing' really quickly and sent it before I lost my nerve, but when I checked again before leaving school, there was still nothing.

It rained this afternoon – heavy, solid rain. The kind of rain that soaks through your clothes in minutes, even if they are meant to be waterproof, that turns gutters into streams and bounces off the ground, and wipes away in seconds the all-night work of a secret street chalk artist. Twig had a match after school (rain doesn't stop rugby), and Dodi was off with Jake. I ran most of the way home on my own, and as my feet hit the sodden pavement my brain kept repeating the excellent question posed by Gloria's pigtailed pupil the day the ponies left the stable under the motorway, 'What's the point?' and I started to feel angry.

What's the point of not answering people when they write to you, like you asked them to?

What's the point of drawing a stupid picture instead?

And what on earth is the point of pictures that disappear?

When I reached the square, I went to his house. I wasn't even nervous when I rang the bell, just cross, but it was nothing to how I feel now. Then I was just cross with Marek for not answering my email, for not telling me straight out that he liked my drawing, for not even talking to me since we stood together on Hungerford Bridge.

Now I am massively, ginormously FURIOUS with the ENTIRE WORLD.

Mrs Valenta opened the door on my second ring. Her eyes were puffy, like she'd been crying.

'Oh,' she said in a tiny, teary voice. 'It's Bluebell, isn't it? I'm afraid now isn't a very good . . .'

Somewhere behind her, two people were yelling at each other.

'I just came . . . I mean, Marek wasn't in school . . .'

Mr Valenta suddenly appeared behind his wife. His face was very red – almost purple, in fact.

'Now is not a good time to talk to Marek,' he informed me.

'Tata!' Marek roared, still out of sight, but Mr Valenta said, 'Goodbye, young lady,' and closed the door in my face.

As I left, I saw the neighbour's curtain twitch.

Twig was in the garden when I got back, standing in the pouring rain in full rugby kit, kicking a football against the wall. Water dripped off his hair and down his neck, and his clothes were so wet they were practically see-through except where they were thick with mud.

'What on earth is going on?' I asked Pixie.

Pixie looked upset and said I had better ask him, so I opened the door and shouted at Twig to come in. He aimed another kick at the football, decapitated a late-flowering geranium and yelled back that he was probably going to stay in the garden for ever.

'But why?'

He kicked the ball again. 'Because …' the ball bounced back – 'of stupid …' he kicked it again – 'stupid, STUPID …' bounce – 'RUGBY!'

The ball sailed into Mrs Henderson's garden. Twig gave a howl of rage.

'What about stupid rugby?' I asked.

'THEY'RE DROPPING ME!' he roared. 'FROM THE TEAM! COACH SAYS I'M NOT GOOD ENOUGH!'

I stepped outside – I was already almost as wet as him anyway – and looked at him more closely.

'Don't cry,' I said.

'I'M NOT CRYING!'

Twig had found an old tennis ball and was hurling that at the wall now instead. Water flew off it every time it hit the brick.

Pixie appeared at the garden door with Pumpkin on her hip. 'Come inside, Twig,' she said, and suddenly all the fight went out of him and he started crying properly.

Jas was sitting in the kitchen when we squelched back in, sticking bits of torn-up red tissue paper on to her geranium painting.

'It's meant to make it more lifelike,' she complained. 'But Mr Boniface doesn't like it. He says he doesn't understand how it relates to the circle of life.'

'How does it?' I asked cautiously.

'I don't know!' Jas wailed. 'I don't even understand what the circle of life is! Do you know what Megan and Chandra and Courtney and Fran are doing? They're going as the four seasons. The four seasons! They're being a living painting. Apparently that exists. Megan's mum is making them each a dress. Courtney is going as an icicle, and Chandra is an oak tree, and Fran is going as an autumn leaf and Megan is going as a daffodil and bringing a lamb.'

'A lamb? In school? In London? In November?'

'Her uncle has a farm and there are lambs on it. And Todd has made a tree out of papier-mâché which is as tall as he is, and he's going to make paper fruit and blossom and birds to hang on it. He says I can share it if I want.'

'Well there you go then,' I said. 'Go and ring him up right now and tell him.'

'I don't want to share Todd's project. They'll say I'm cheating and also that he's my boyfriend. I hate school. I just want to die and never go back ever again.'

And then she burst into tears.

Later, when everyone had stopped crying and was dry and warm again, and Pixie had cooked a huge dish of spaghetti and Jas had taken Pumpkin into bed with her to read him a story, and I was trying to do my homework but actually thinking about Marek, Twig came into my room and slumped on the end of my bed.

'I'm sorry about the team,' I told him. 'Though it was kind of obvious you weren't really enjoying it.'

Twig said, 'It is extremely difficult in this family to admit that you're not good at anything.'

He picked at my duvet while I thought about this.

'Everybody is so brilliant at everything,' he went on when I didn't say anything. 'It's all, oh Blue is a secret film genius and isn't Jas a marvellous poet and Flora's going to be a star.'

'But you're clever,' I said. 'You're so clever. And none of us are brilliant, you know. Flora's play is awful, and Jas is a terrible artist, and there is really no way I am a genius.'

'I don't care about being clever!' Twig cried. 'That's only good for school. I want to be good at something else.'

I felt completely helpless. 'Maybe sport just isn't your thing,' I suggested.

Twig announced he was giving up and shuffled away to his bedroom.

But Marek not talking to me and Jas crying about the cupcake girls and Twig crying over rugby and even Mr Valenta closing the door in my face are not the reason I am so angry.

The reason I am massively, ginormously FURIOUS with the ENTIRE WORLD is this.

Marek did answer my email, eventually. His reply to my question, 'Are you OK?' was just one line.

'No,' Marek wrote. 'I am not OK. Dad found out about the drawings, and they are sending me to Wales.'

Marek's leaving at the end of next week.

He didn't even come to school today. Mr Valenta says he has to carry on going to Clarendon Free until he goes, but I guess Marek doesn't care what his father says any more because when I came home he was waiting for me sitting on our wall, wearing a sweatshirt covered in chalk dust and a miserable expression on his face.

'Can I come in?' he asked.

I don't know what Marek makes of the difference between his house and ours. I noticed every chip and scuff and stain on the walls on the way down to the kitchen, but when I glanced at him he was still wearing exactly the same scowl, and not looking at anything at all.

It was the picture of the miniature dachshund that did it, he said.

'Violet's been going on about it for ages,' he told me as I made us tea. 'I knew it was kind of stupid when I did it, but I couldn't resist. I feel so sorry for that dog. She's always yanking his lead and it's not good for dachshunds to be so fat, because they have very sensitive backs. Anyway, she has been looking for the culprit – that's what she said, culprit not artist – for ages. At first she thought it was you, because of the drawings you did in your front garden, but Mrs Henderson told her it couldn't possibly be, because none of you were good enough. She's been sniffing around searching for clues, and then yesterday morning...'

He stopped to draw breath. 'I'm so stupid,' he said. 'I'm normally so careful.'

'What happened yesterday morning?' I asked.

It was the poor little fat dachshund again, being taken out for his morning walk. How was Marek to know Violet Doriot-Buffet's husband always went out so early? That he didn't just let the dog into the garden, but took it out for a jog (or in the case of the dachshund, waddle) around the block? Marek usually gets home much earlier from his night-time drawing sessions, and he usually always covers his chalk-covered clothes with a coat in case anyone sees him. But his father was up late working on the night of the Hungerford Bridge picture, and Marek fell asleep. He didn't sneak out until after four o'clock in the morning, the drawing took a long time to get right and it was cold that night too. He kept his coat on, and it got covered in dust.

It turns out I was right about one thing: a chalk

artist, after spending many hours drawing, is a very multi-coloured sight, and impossible to ignore.

Marek passed Mr Doriot-Buffet in the street, just round the corner from the Hungerford Bridge drawing. Mr Doriot-Buffet saw Marek, saw the picture, realised who had drawn the picture of his dog doing a poo, put two and two together, and told his wife as soon as she woke up, and she went straight over before breakfast to tell the Valentas.

'I've no doubt the police will want to get involved,' Mrs Doriot-Buffet said, when she told Marek's parents their son had been busy vandalising public property all over the neighbourhood and also, incidentally, that she always cleaned up after her dog.

'And so that was that,' Marek said. 'Dad went ballistic, Mum cried and I am off to Wales. I didn't think he'd actually go through with it after the argument we had, but he rang them first thing and they said I can start immediately. Tata's over the moon. He ordered the whole uniform online himself, cross-country running shoes and all.'

'But you can't go if you don't want to!' I cried.

'You try telling Tata that.'

For once, there was nobody in the kitchen. Marek absently took a chalk out of his pocket and started to draw with it on the table. A mountain appeared as I watched, and then a little figure, trudging uphill with a bag on his back.

'I thought your film was awesome, Blue.'

Something swelled up inside me then, growing bigger and bigger till I thought I was going to burst, but this time it wasn't happiness that he liked my film, but sadness for him.

'Has your dad actually seen your drawings?' I asked. 'Does he know how good you are?'

'It wouldn't change anything even if he had,' Marek said.

The chalks I bought from the toy shop were still sitting where we left them weeks ago on the dresser. I selected a pink one at random, and drew a daisy on the table.

'I draw like a three-year-old,' I told him. 'I could practise for a lifetime and never be as good as you.'

Marek smiled. Then, with one swipe of his sleeve, he rubbed out all the drawings.

*

I went upstairs after Marek left. Flora and Dad were arguing in his study. Next door in Pumpkin's room, Pixie was singing him lullabies and wearing her wings.

'What's going on?' I asked.

Pixie said Flora's play had closed, just like Dad said it would. 'Your father wants Flora to go back to Scotland. The school have agreed to take her back. Flora doesn't want to go.'

I stuck my head outside to listen.

'But I have PAID for this,' Dad was saying.

'I don't NEED drama school!' Flora pleaded.

'Well what else are you going to do?'

'How long have they been arguing?' I asked Pixie. She said about half an hour, and that she was trying to rise above it. She made a fluttering motion with her hands like she was flying. I laughed and she looked pleased.

'You see,' she said. 'They do work. You came in with a face like a rainy day, but now the sun's come out. All because of a pair of fairy wings.'

Pixie is barking mad but I think I might actually love her.

Upstairs again in her bedroom, Jas was sticking real flower petals on her geranium collage.

'Why?' I asked.

'To make it look more alive.' She had a sort of manic look in her eyes. 'Do you think it's working?'

I looked at it carefully. It was an even worse mess than before.

'Absolutely,' I said.

'You're lying. If you really did think it was working, you wouldn't have asked why I was doing it.'

She sighed and jabbed more glue at her painting, so hard she punctured it.

'They're going to win, aren't they? Megan and Courtney and Chandra and Fran and their stupid lamb and living picture. I couldn't even stand up and recite a poem.'

Twig was lying on the floor on the other side of the room, watching rugby videos on my laptop.

'He thinks they'll help,' Jas said. 'He's going to beg the coach to give him a second chance. I don't see why he would. He hasn't scored a single goal all term.'

'You score tries in rugby, not goals,' Twig informed her. 'And at least I'm not weird.'

'Twig!' I cried.

'Well, I'm sorry!' Twig stomped out of the room.

'Don't listen to him,' I told Jas.

'No, he's right.' A large tear rolled down along Jas's nose and plopped on to her picture. 'I am weird. Everybody thinks so.'

There were footsteps running up the stairs and along the landing, and Flora's bedroom door slammed shut.

'You can go if you want,' Jas said. 'There's nothing

you can do for me.'

Flora was lying in bed with all her clothes on and the duvet pulled over her head.

'Go away,' she said.

'I just wanted to make sure you're all right.'

'Of course I'm not all right.'

She sat up. The duvet fell away. Her face was one big puffy smudge of eye makeup, with hair plastered to her face on the side she had been lying on, and sticking up everywhere else. She looked like an electrocuted zombie.

'I suppose you heard the play's finished,' she said. 'And that Dad is trying to banish me.'

'Not banish,' I said. 'It's not Shakespeare. It's just Scotland.'

'I don't want to go back!'

'But I thought you liked it. Maud and Peter and Barney, walking around the countryside in your nightdress, and everyone wearing wings.'

Flora was lying on her side with her head on her hands and her knees drawn up to her chest. She looked nothing like the Flora who strode down Plumpton High Street planning Halloween parades, or who marched around Chatsworth Square carrying flaming torches, or looked radiant and triumphant as she took her bow in the theatre, believing she was a great success. She looked about twelve years old.

'It's not your fault about the play,' I told her. 'I bet if Angel had made it normal instead of doing all that weird space stuff, everyone would have said you were amazing. You are amazing.'

'I'm not.' Her eyes welled up again. I handed her a tissue. And then she told me.

The reason Flora doesn't want to go back to drama school isn't that she thinks she's too good.

It's that she thinks she isn't good enough.

'Barney's a great actor,' Flora said. 'He can literally do anything. And Peter's not a great actor, but he's brilliant at directing. And Maud – well, you've seen Maud. She's mesmerising. She doesn't even have to open her mouth. She could just stand on a stage pretending to be a tree and you wouldn't want to watch anyone else. I did Angel's play to prove I was better than them, and now I just look like an idiot.'

'I bet you're just as good as them.'

Flora smiled, just a tiny smile, and said please could she have a hug, so I climbed into bed with her.

'It's so scary,' she whispered, when we were lying cuddled up under the duvet. 'It was different when I was at school. It was easy to be the best then. But at drama school, everyone's the best. Except me.'

It was nice lying together in Flora's bed. Night was falling outside, and there were no lights on in her room. In the growing dark, my mind drifted.

'I've got a friend,' I told Flora. 'His dad wants to send him to boarding school.'

'A boyfriend?' Flora asked sleepily.

'No!' I protested, thankful for the darkness, but Flora can always detect what she calls feelings, even when she's in the pit of misery herself. She raised herself on to an elbow to look at me.

'Who is he?'

'It's only Marek Valenta!' I mumbled. 'You know – he came for drinks with his parents.'

'Oh, him.' Flora sounded disappointed. 'What about him?'

'I was just thinking. Neither of you wants to leave.'

But Flora was no longer interested. She closed her eyes, and soon her breath turned into snores.

Yesterday, I thought that all I wanted was for Marek to like my film. Today I keep thinking about what Mum said when we were emptying the stables – how the most important thing is for us all to be happy. And I think I have sat back and not done anything for too long. I've stood by while Jas got bullied, and I've watched Twig try and try to be good at something he hated, and I've let Flora believe her play was brilliant when maybe it might have been better to try and convince her to go back to drama school.

Well, I've had enough of sitting back. I don't care if nobody wants my help.

I crept out of her bed to my room, and called Dodi.

'I'm just waiting for Jake to call,' she said.

'I need to talk.'

And, despite being so taken up with Jake, Dodi is still a good friend, because I talked to her for ages and despite Jake trying to call her four times while we were on the phone, she didn't answer him once.

I told her everything. About Marek being the chalk artist, and the boarding school in Wales, and going to the National Gallery and Marek's feather-light kiss. I told her about sending Marek my video and going crazy waiting for a reply, and what the drawing of Hungerford Bridge meant to me.

'What did it mean?'

'That he liked my video. That he likes me. That we're ... I think, that we both see the world the same way.'

'Do you like him?' Dodi asked.

'Yes,' I said. 'I do. I like him a lot.'

Even as I said that, I realised how true it was. I can't remember ever liking someone so much.

'Everything's rubbish,' I told her. 'I haven't told you about my family yet.'

'So let me sum this up,' Dodi said when I'd finished. 'Flora wants to be an actress but thinks she's not good enough, Jas has been crushed by those cupcake fiends, Twig's in a state because he thinks he's hopeless at everything, you're miserable because the boy you love ...'

'I didn't say love!'

'The boy you like is going away, and he's a mess because he's going away.'

There was a pause. 'Do you think my family's out of control?' I asked.

'I think your family's barking,' Dodi said. 'The question is, what are you going to do about it?'

Wednesday 17 November

I have been thinking about Marek's last drawing. Not the big, wonderful Hungerford Bridge, but the little figure on the kitchen table, trudging up the hill. I know that figure was supposed to be Marek, but it could just as well be any of us. Sad, crushed, tiny people struggling up hills. And I have been thinking that this is not us.

We are not like we were after Iris died. We are not sad, crushed, tiny people.

I have also been thinking about Pixie. Pixie and her hair and her wings and her yoga, who was brave enough to leave a town in Ireland where everyone knew who she was to live in a town where she knew nobody, who is a tiny bit ridiculous but who doesn't care what people think of her.

And I also have been thinking about Angel and his terrible production of *Romeo and Juliet*, and of what that nice reviewer said, that it was possible one day he might do something good because he has a big imagination and isn't afraid to use it.

The Pixies and Angels of this world are right. Being afraid is pointless.

Now that the weather is colder, Pixie has started doing her morning yoga in the kitchen instead of the garden. Mum was funny about it at first because she said it interfered with everyone's breakfast, but the kitchen is big, Pixie is small, Mum's usually left by the time she starts and Pumpkin absolutely loves it. He sits on his own play mat next to her yoga mat and laughs at her, while she stands with her hands in the air, then does all these super-energetic lunges and bends and stretches, pulling silly faces at him all the time she is doing it.

'I thought yoga was supposed to be all calm,' I said this morning.

'Doesn't mean it can't be fun,' Pixie said. 'Anyway, this is just to wake me up in the morning. The exercises are called Sun Salutations.' She laughed. 'We should get Jas to do them for her art project. Night, day, day, night, the sun rising every morning. That's the circle of life, right? She could paint her face like she did with Todd, one half moon and the other half sun.'

And that is when it struck me.

Jas's art project. A solution to everyone's problems. Well, to Jas and Marek's, anyway. And maybe Flora's. Maybe even Twig's . . .

'Pixie,' I said. 'You're a genius.'

Twig dragged his sports bag to school this morning like it was filled with bricks rather than shorts and shirts and boots, and Jas was dressed completely in grey – Twig's old grey jumper over her faded leggings and under an old grey coat, a grey gingham headband holding back her hair and grubby grey trainers. She looked like a very scruffy pigeon. Nobody talked. I was thinking. Twig and Jas were just consumed by gloom.

My plan, if it comes off, will be . . . spectacular. Epic. Technicolour.

Marek is still not at school. I spent most of this morning's lessons making sketches in my exercise books. Then at lunchtime, I went to find Twig and took him aside to show him what I was thinking and to explain how we could make it happen.

'It's crazy,' he said. 'Also, impossible.'

'We've done crazy impossible things before.'

'We don't know what we're doing and we'd need loads of people.'

'I know exactly what I'm doing,' I said. 'And what about the rugby team?'

'No flipping way. Not when I'm trying to get back on the team'.

'Twig! Think how much they loved Halloween!'

'Fine,' Twig grumbled. 'I'll talk to them.'

After speaking to Twig I stopped in the library to use a computer. I checked the weather forecast for the next five days on as many weather-predicting websites as I could find.

Scattered showers till the end of the week, fair at the weekend and going into Monday.

Perfect weather for a gang of secret chalk artists.

As soon as school finished, I ran round to the primary school. I caught Jas just as she was coming out. She shuffled out past the four cupcake girls with her eyes on the ground. One of them laughed – Courtney, I think. Jas didn't even look up.

'Come on.' I took her arm and dragged her back into school, pulling my camera out of my bag.

'What are you doing?'

'I need to photograph every inch of this playground.'

'Why?'

Her eyes got bigger and bigger as I explained.

'No,' she said when I'd finished.

'Jas!'

'No!'

An angel appeared, wearing a bow tie.

'Hello, Blue,' said Todd.

I told him my plan.

'Yes,' said Todd. 'Yes, yes, yes, yes, yes.'

Jas said, 'It will be like Halloween all over again. Or like the poetry reading. You thought that was a good idea too! It'll be like Halloween AND the poetry reading.'

'Exactly!' I said. 'Only this time, I promise nothing will go wrong.'

Even though I know it isn't actually physically possible, I swear Todd grew at least two inches.

'Don't worry, Blue,' he said, grasping hold of Jas's hand. 'I'll convince her.'

Back home, I stole Flora's phone to get Peter's number. I talked to him for ages.

All I need now is to convince Marek.

Thursday 18 November

We met in the gardens in the square. I wanted to be absolutely sure no-one could overhear us, so we sat on the grass right in the middle of the lawn. Marek listened very carefully to my plan. I'm sure I even detected a flicker of interest and possibly even of admiration, but when it came to the question, 'Will you do it?' his response was very clear.

'This plan is insane,' he said.

'But you've got nothing to lose!'

'Excuse me, I have everything to lose!' he protested. 'What if Tata finds out?'

'The whole point of this is for your dad to find out,' I said. 'For him to see what you can do.'

'If I did this – this thing, and if Tata found out, he probably wouldn't even let me come home for the holidays. He would make me stay at St Llwydian all year round, and forbid them from giving me so much as a pencil. He would probably break all my fingers so I could never draw again. You don't know what he's like.'

I thought of Mr Valenta, purple-faced and slamming his front door in my face. Mr Valenta in our house, showing off his expensive clothes, and Mr Valenta at the theatre in his expensive car.

Then I thought of Mr Valenta driving past our house during the party before Flora's play, his face so sad.

'He might surprise you,' I said softly.

'It's over, Blue.' Marek sat with his arms wrapped round his knees, the picture of tiny crushed miserableness. 'Tata's won. He'll never let me go to art college, and he'll never let me do what I want. It's sweet of you to try, but . . .'

'I'm not being sweet!'

Sweet made me bubble with anger and disappointment.

Sweet is even worse than sensible.

'It's not sweet to stand up for yourself,' I told him. 'Or to fight for what you want. It's . . . it's brave, and defiant and strong.'

'That's just stories,' Marek said.

'It's not!' I insisted. 'Look at me and Dodi!'

'Dodi?'

'She was always bossing me about and telling me what to do. But I stood up to her . . .'

I trailed off. I still don't like remembering how I stood up to Dodi, or how wrong that could have gone.

'And what happened?' Marek asked.

'Things changed,' I said. 'And we're still friends. You've got to stand up to him, Marek. You can't just give up your dreams like he did. You've got to show him how much it matters to you. If you don't, how is he ever going to understand you?'

Marek rested his forehead on his knees so I couldn't see his face. For a minute, I thought that he was going to cry. Then he unfolded himself and got up without another word.

'It's been great knowing you, Blue,' he mumbled.

He walked away. Suddenly I felt furious again.

'You're just scared!' I yelled after him.

But he didn't turn around.

Todd was waiting at our house when I got home, playing with Flora's old makeup while Jas stuck dead leaves on her geranium collage and Twig did a nature magazine crossword.

'Well?' Todd asked when I came in. 'What did he say?'

I shook my head.

'Probably just as well,' Twig said.

He's miserable because Coach has said no to a second chance.

'Not just as well,' Todd said. 'Not just as well at all.'

'I have no more solutions,' I told them, and went to bed.

I have tried to help. I have tried to be brave and ambitious and come up with the sort of solution you would get in a film, where whole communities are saved by pulling together and putting aside their differences, and audiences come out feeling that anything is possible, but now I have run out of ideas and it is very, very sad.

Flora came in to see me. 'So,' she said. 'I saw you and the posh boy in the square.'

'Did you?' I said.

'He is your boyfriend.'

'He really isn't.'

'But you want him to be.'

I love Flora, I honestly do, and I feel sorry for her and everything, but she is the most annoying person in the world.

'You are perfectly absurd,' I told her. 'Now please go away and never talk to me again.'

I called Zoran in Devon.

'How do you make someone do something they don't want to do?'

'You don't,' he said. 'What are you up to now?'

I told him my plan. 'Don't you think it's brilliant?'

'No,' Zoran said. 'I think it's crazy and I'm not surprised people don't want to do it.'

I said goodbye, because I am tired of people telling me I'm crazy, and called Skye instead.

'It's not crazy,' Skye said. 'It's big. That's not the same as crazy.'

I love Skye.

'And you can't do it without this Marek guy?'

'We really can't. He's a proper artist. Without him it'd all just be mess. And anyway, I wanted to help him too. It's supposed to help everybody.'

Skye said that was a shame, and then he changed the subject and said seriously, Blue, was it true that horrible girl who's been bullying Jas was bringing a lamb to school?

'Seriously,' I said.

'That's mental,' he said.

'Yes.'

'And cruel to animals.'

'Welcome to the Cupcake Crew.'

Skye went quiet and then he said, 'I wish I could help you,' and I said, 'That's nice but you can't because you're in Devon,' and we both said goodbye.

The last person I called was Peter.

'It's all off,' I told him.

'We'll come anyway,' he said. 'Just don't tell Flora yet.'

Sunday 21 November

There was a bad atmosphere at home until the drama students came. I stayed in bed. The others spent most of the day in Flora's room, whispering, probably about me.

The doorbell rang and it was Barney and Peter and Maud. Mum shouted up the stairs for Flora to come down. Flora said what for, and then there was the sound of three people coming up the stairs, all 'Flora, Flora wherefore art thou Flora,' which is what Juliet famously says to Romeo. I thought that was a bit tactless but then I heard Flora fling open her door and shout, 'You guys!' and they were all falling into each other's arms and hugging and kissing, and Maud and Peter and Barney were all, 'Darling, bad luck about the show but you have to come back,' and Flora was,

'I can't' and they were all, 'But sweetheart you must, I swear it's dead up there without you.' And then Flora said, 'I'll think about it' and they all squealed and my bedroom door was flung open and Flora said, 'Blue, did you ask these guys to come?' and I said, 'maybe' and they all jumped on my bed and tickled me until I had to scream for them to get off.

'Dearest,' Peter said, tucking his arm behind my head. 'Why so glum?'

'Blue's in love,' Flora informed them.

'*Pauvre petite*,' crooned Maud.

'That means "poor little you",' Barney told me. 'We're doing *The Three Musketeers* next term and now Maud only speaks French.'

'I am NOT in love,' I said.

'Get out of bed then and come and plot,' Peter said.

'Thank you,' I said. 'But I am thinking of staying in bed for ever.'

I checked my email about a thousand times, but there were no messages from Marek.

Everything is over.

All afternoon, people tramped up and down stairs to Flora's room with cups of tea and packets of biscuits. Jas and Twig were there. Pumpkin too, when Mum and Dad went out, after his nap. Pixie came home from her yoga class and joined in as well. The phone rang a lot, and the front door slammed quite a few times too.

It got dark. I thought of watching my videos, but couldn't find my camera. I watched TV shows on my laptop instead. Eventually, I pulled on a sweatshirt over my pyjamas and shuffled into Flora's room. There were people everywhere – on the bed, on the floor, at her desk.

Every single one of them looked guilty.

Pixie said she had to get supper. Maud said she had to practise the *trompette*. Jas drooped tragically and said she had to put the finishing touches to her dead leaf picture for the art show tomorrow – not that anyone would notice it – and Twig sighed and had better do his homework, since there was nothing else in his life now.

They all dispersed.

'What's going on?' I asked Flora.

'Nothing!' she said brightly, and I have never been more certain that she was lying.

Monday 22 November

It's three o'clock in the morning. Something just woke me – a noise, like people moving about. I went out on to the landing, but everything was quiet. I looked out at the street but there was nothing there. I'm back in bed now, writing to make myself not be afraid.

I must have dozed off with the light. There was another noise. A creak on the stairs, a bump, a muffled curse.

Someone was in the house.

This time I didn't dare get up. I lay flat in bed and pulled the duvet around me. 'I'm imagining things,' I told myself. 'There's no-one there.'

The steps drew nearer.

My bedroom door creaked open. I opened my mouth to scream, but someone was already leaping across the room, so fast I couldn't see him, and was right beside me with his hand over my mouth.

I bit the hand. Its owner yelped. His smell, his voice, everything about him was familiar.

'Shut up,' whispered Skye. 'Don't wake your parents.'

'What are you doing?' I hissed, when he removed his hand.

'I've come to get you. Quick, get dressed. Warm clothes, it's freezing outside. I'll wait on the landing.'

In front of the house, Zoran sat at the wheel of a horsebox.

'What...'

'Don't ask,' he said.

From the horsebox behind us came the sound of a plaintive whinny. Skye grinned, his glasses more crooked than ever.

'A pony's way more impressive than a lamb,' he said. 'Come on, let's go!'

'Where?'

'Where do you think? It's Monday morning. School, of course.'

The Film Diaries of Bluebell Gadsby

Scene Thirteen
A Pony Really Is Way More Impressive than a Lamb

Clarendon Free Primary School, just before dawn. The playground is full of people - much fuller than it should be when it is still dark, the gates aren't yet open and school is officially closed. They have been busy for hours, but the lightening sky gives a new sense of urgency to their movements. They flit like shadows through the playground, on ladders, on windowsills, on benches, flat on their bellies on the ground, all at the bidding of a central figure, ring-master, choreographer and director of operations: MAREK VALENTA, coat flung open, shirt tails flying and hair any which way, with coloured chalk all over his hands and a smile plastered over his face.

In the darkest corner of the yard, surrounded by high walls that stop the sound of a fiddle from travelling beyond the school confines, FLORA and MAUD, their faces and hands alarmingly painted to resemble the leaves and branches of trees, practise a dance routine. Off camera, a pony whinnies.

Hands clasped to her chest, chin held high, JASMINE stands alone in the middle of the yard, reciting poetry.

The sun rises.

The forecasters were right. It will be a beautiful day.

CAMERAMAN
It's getting light. We should go.

Fourteen rugby players, three drama students, one ex-nanny, Flora, TWIG, SKYE, DODI, JAKE, TOM and COLIN – climb one by one over the school gates. Only Jasmine and Marek remain. Alone, they pace the playground for one final check before making for the gates themselves.

Marek half smiles at the camera before he slips away.

All vanish homewards, to wash and eat and change before returning to school an hour later, uncharacteristically early, to witness at first hand the Grand Opening of the Year Six Annual Art Project: The Circle of Life.

Jas's display was spectacular.

People will be talking about what we did today for years. For ever, maybe. It was A WORK OF BEAUTY.

My work of beauty. My bonkers, ambitious, completely unsensible idea for a fabulous feel-good ending.

'I called Jas,' Skye said in the horsebox this morning on the way to school. 'I said how brilliant your plan was and how we had to do it. I said, I know how scary it will be, but we would all be there to help her. Then that kid Todd got involved.'

'That was Twig's idea,' Zoran said. 'He thought the smallest people would be the most convincing, and that Jas and Todd together should go and talk to Marek. He's obviously as crazy as the rest of you, because he was already having second thoughts. Then when Todd and Jas turned up on his doorstep, telling him how badly they were being picked on at school ... well, I think your Marek is a nice person, as well as mad, because he agreed immediately.'

'Twig's kind of a genius, sending those two,' Skye said. 'Jas and Todd together – I don't think anyone could resist them. I tell you, he'll be running the country one day.'

We pulled into the parking bay in front of the primary school.

'So we're doing it,' I breathed.

Zoran glanced over and smiled. 'Just don't tell Gloria, OK?'

I was first in line when the school gates opened, with my camera in my jacket. We figured the school wouldn't let us in all at once without questioning us. Flora came next with Maud, with hats pulled low over their made-up faces, then Barney, Peter, Twig and Todd and finally Marek and Zoran.

Skye and Jas saved their entrance for later.

I filmed everything. Everything.

A star-spangled night sky of indigo and silver. A sunset of purple and orange. A dawn of rose and yellow and purple. A summer's day of blazing gold and blue, a snowstorm on a winter landscape, rain falling from fluffy clouds on to green rolling countryside. The astonished faces of hundreds of children as they walked into school and found it transformed from brick and concrete and tarmac into an explosion of colour. Some of the drawings were better than others, but it didn't matter. Night, day, summer, winter: the circle of life covered every inch of that playground, and all together they formed a perfect salutation to the new dawn.

Maybe it was too much when Barney struck up his violin and Flora and Maud threw off their coats and hats and started to dance around a small papier-mâché tree hung with paper birds and fruits and flowers. Except that if they hadn't started the dance, others wouldn't have joined in. Lots of others. Little kids joined hands with Flora and Maud and danced in a circle round the tree while older kids stood by and watched as the violin went faster and faster, until even the teachers started to tap their feet and clap.

It was definitely too much for Jas to turn up on Mopsy, bareback with a crown of flowers in her hair, reciting her 'Circle of Life' poem through a megaphone stolen from the secondary school rugby coach. I'm not sure anyone could hear the words, but I don't think that matters. And oh, the look on Megan's face when she turned up in a long flowery pink frock, dragging a lamb on a lead!

I remembered what Dodi said about Halloween being all about Flora, and that Jas should be normal. The last thing Jas could or should ever be is normal. This morning, as she recited poetry on horseback, it was all about her. And Skye is so right. A pony is way more impressive than a lamb.

Megan saw the pony and dropped the lead. The lamb, who was having a horrible time and had no idea what it was doing in London, let alone a school, ran away, scattering droppings as it went. Skye caught it and became an instant star attraction with children wanting to pet it.

Ms Smokey started shouting about health and safety but nobody listened.

Kids passing the gates on their way to the secondary school stopped and took photographs on their phones. The local paper, seeing, 'Farm Animals Run Wild in West London Primary School' trending on Twitter, sent a reporter to cover the story. The crowds grew bigger and bigger. Ms Smokey gave up on starting a normal school day and asked people to form an orderly queue instead. 'Viewing of this exceptional art installation will be time-limited to five minutes per visitor,' she shouted into a loudspeaker, and also, 'All cash donations will be gratefully received.'

The under-fourteen rugby team turned up (by now, loads of the secondary school were here). The captain informed the local paper that rugby players made excellent artists, and also that Twig, though a really terrible rugby player, was awesome at telling people what to do. The team picked him up and carried him around the playground on their shoulders.

Twig turned scarlet.

Everything has to end, I suppose. Eventually the police arrived to find out what all the fuss was about and, after admiring the chalk paintings, asked everyone to start moving along now please. The headmaster stormed over from the secondary school to find out why half his students hadn't turned up for morning lessons. People remembered they had to go to work, and drifted back to the morning bustle of Blenheim Avenue. Mr Boniface remembered that other pupils had also contributed to the art project and deserved attention.

The playground emptied. Jas slipped off Mopsy, hugged us all, and ran into school with Todd to the sound of her classmates' cheers.

Nobody paid any attention to Megan, Courtney, Chandra and Fran.

Skye and Zoran led Mopsy back to the horsebox, together with the lamb. The caretaker leaned on his broom beside me, surveying a pile of pony droppings. He looked at the chalk paintings one by one, and his grumpy face turned into a reluctant smile.

'Suppose the rain'll clear that lot away in due course,' he said.

'It will,' I promised. 'And the forecast's wet for tonight.'

Flora, Maud and Peter stopped dancing and walked towards the gates, talking loudly about coffee. Barney didn't follow. Eyes closed, lost in his own world, he stood alone by Todd's tree in the middle of the playground, still playing his fiddle.

'He's playing Tchaikovsky,' Peter said. 'You don't interrupt Barney when he plays Tchaikovsky. Tell him where we've gone, Blue, will you?'

And then, apart from the caretaker sweeping in his corner and Barney playing with his eyes closed, only Marek and I were left.

We walked towards each other from opposite sides of the playground. Marek ran his hands through hair so dusty with chalk it practically stood upright, and when he smiled it was the proper smile I saw on Hungerford Bridge.

'We did it,' he said.

'*You* did it.'

'We *all* did it.'

And now we were standing right in front of each other. Barney's playing was getting faster and faster, building to a finale. Marek reached out both hands for mine and we started to spin like a couple of kids.

'We did it!' I shouted, but Marek didn't shout back.

He slowed down. He stopped spinning. I staggered to a halt and followed the direction of his gaze, to the entrance gates which were deserted now except for one person.

Mr Valenta – tailored-suited, cashmere-coated, custom shod and hatted – stood stony-faced beside his wife on the edge of the playground, surveying his son's work.

'What's he doing here?' Marek asked.

'I may have had a word with your mum,' I admitted.

Time froze. Nobody moved. There was no sound except for the violin.

'This was a disaster,' I thought.

And then Marek was walking across the playground, with his crazy hair and his clothes full of multi-coloured chalk dust. He stood before his father and held out a piece of chalk.

'You did this?' Mr Valenta asked.

He spoke very carefully, like he was daring Marek to admit that he had. Like he might explode if he did. And then Mrs Valenta put her hand on his arm, and a look passed between them, and it was like when they came for drinks, when she told us that he used to be a great violinist.

'Tell him, Marek,' she said quietly.

'Just because you could not play the violin ...' Marek's voice shook. He paused, swallowed, and started again. 'It doesn't mean I can't be an artist. It's what I love more than anything in the world, and if you stop me, it will be like killing me.'

Mr Valenta opened his mouth. Mrs Valenta squeezed his arm, and he closed it.

'I want to be an artist.' Marek was sounding much firmer now. 'But I don't want to do it in secret. I want to do it out in the open, and I want you to be proud of me.'

As Marek spoke, Mr Valenta's face changed from a glare to a frown to the sort of crumpled look people get when they are trying not to cry.

'Well?' Marek's voice wobbled again. 'Aren't you going to say something?'

Mr Valenta opened his arms, and Marek fell straight into them.

They stayed for ages. Mr and Mrs Valenta walked around the playground with Marek, looking at all the drawings, but I didn't go with them. I sat on a wall and watched and smiled, because as they walked and looked Mr Valenta's tie seemed to come looser too, and his Paris hat sat at a jauntier angle. He reached out to touch one of the drawings, His coat brushed against the wall and came away covered in chalk. And all the time, Barney kept on playing, softly, softly, until Ms Smokey came out to ask us to please go away once and for all.

Barney packed his fiddle away and went to join the others in the café. Mr Valenta went to work, still dabbing at his eyes. Mrs Valenta kissed us both and went with him.

'Wow.' Marek looked dazed.

'I told you it was a good plan,' I said.

'It was the violin that did it. That was a stroke of genius. It reminded him what it was like. What he used to be like.'

I smiled modestly, because there's no denying it. Getting Barney to play the violin was a brilliant idea.

'Did he say anything about Wales?' I asked.

'Tata? No. But Mum said before she left that we would talk this weekend.'

'The violin,' I admitted, 'was sort of a fluke.'

Then neither of us knew quite what to say.

'I guess we'd better go to school,' I said.

'I guess.'

There is a tiny piece of green between the primary and secondary, just big enough for a couple of benches and a few bushes tall enough to hide them. And there are times when life is just too big for school.

We stopped at the green and sat on one of the benches and we talked and talked and talked.

At one point, Marek took my hand in his. And he didn't let go.

Once I had a twin sister called Iris. She was like half of me. I loved her more than anyone else in the world, and when she died I thought I would never be happy again. My diaries then were all about her. Oh, not just her. They were about all of us, the people we met, the things we did – and we have done a lot. But all the same, at the heart of them there was me, missing Iris.

Now it's different.

It's not that I don't still love her, and miss her, and wish that she was here every single day. It's just – it's not at the centre of everything any more. It's more of a shadow in the corner of the room. I know she's there, watching me. I know she loves me. I know she doesn't mind.

The most important thing is for us all to be happy. I know it's what she wants too.

Jas didn't win the art prize. Mr Boniface thanked her for bringing joy and colour to the school (his words), but said that with so many people involved who didn't actually attend Clarendon Free Primary, he couldn't honestly give the prize to her. He gave it to Todd instead, which was perfect. As Jas said, the whole point was for Megan and Courtney and Chandra and Fran not to win, and obviously they didn't. Jas and Todd were their school heroes for about week. Then other things happened, the way things do in school, and people began to forget about them. Jas doesn't mind though. She says she doesn't care about being popular, as long as people just leave her alone. She has given up art for ever and has started writing a novel in verse. At the weekends, she and Todd get together and make clothes.

Twig has given up on sport and taken up debating instead. He's pretty good at it.

Flora is back at drama school. She called yesterday, super-excited because she's got herself an agent. 'Next stop Broadway!' she cried. 'Or Hollywood! I don't know yet which I'd rather.'

Dad said quite sternly that before becoming a star, she must first learn to be an actor, but Flora said Dad didn't understand a thing.

Pumpkin took his first steps. I wish I could say it was towards one of us, but actually it was towards Pixie, or more precisely towards the cookie she was holding out to him. I filmed it. It's the sweetest, funniest thing I've ever seen, especially the bit where he crams the whole cookie in his mouth.

Marek didn't go to Wales. He talked about it for ages with his parents – properly, without shouting – and they agreed to let him stay at Clarendon Free (as long as his grades don't suffer). He has stopped doing his chalk drawings and is doing art at school now. He spends every weekend squirrelled away in different galleries, drawing. Sometimes I go with him, sometimes I don't. Sometimes, if you pass his house at night and stop to listen, you can hear a violin.

Down in Devon, Zoran is composing a musical. He says it's based on all of us. And after a long winter, Grandma says she's well enough to help Gloria with the horses. 'Just a bit of grooming,' she says. Skye says Gloria's horses are the best brushed in the whole of Devon.

I applied for the film course Peter told me about. It took me a while to work up to it but in the end I decided to go for it, because what's the point of making art that no-one gets to see? The letter came this morning, telling me I've got a place. It's a summer course, so it means that for the first time in my life I won't be spending the holidays in Devon. I was sad at first, but it's all right. Devon and Grandma and Skye and the others will all still be there when I've finished. Making films is what I have always wanted to do.

One day, I'll make history.

Life's just getting started.